PRAISE FOR
RACHAEL HERRON'S
WORK

"A poignant, profound ode to the enduring and redemptive power of love."

– Library Journal

"A celebration of the power of love to heal even the most broken of hearts."

- NYT Bestselling Author Susan Wiggs

"A heart-warming story of family, friendship and love in a town you'll never want to leave."

– Barbara Freethy, USA Today Bestseller

ALSO BY RACHAEL HERRON

FICTION:

STANDALONE NOVELS:

THE ONES WHO MATTER MOST
SPLINTERS OF LIGHT
PACK UP THE MOON

THE DARLING BAY NOVELS
THE DARLING SONGBIRDS
THE SONGBIRD'S CALL
THE SONGBIRD SISTERS
And don't miss the Firefighters (4 books)
and the Ballard Brothers of Darling Bay (3 books) series!

CYPRESS HOLLOW NOVELS 1-5:

HOW TO KNIT A LOVE SONG
HOW TO KNIT A HEART BACK HOME
WISHES & STITCHES
CORA'S HEART
FIONA'S FLAME

MEMOIR:

A LIFE IN STITCHES

Build it Strong

by

RACHAEL HERRON

Publisher's Note: This is a work of fiction. Names, characters, places, and incidents are a product of the author's imagination. Locales and public names are sometimes used for atmospheric purposes. Any resemblance to actual people, living or dead, or to businesses, companies, events, institutions, or locales is completely coincidental.

On the Market / Rachael Herron. -- 1st ed.

HGA Publishing

ISBN-13: 978-1-940785-34-9

BUILD IT STRONG

CHAPTER ONE

A idan couldn't have been in a blacker mood if the earth had stopped rotating, leaving California's coast in perpetual darkness. He pulled up in front of the old Callahan house with a roar of tires, a spray of gravel, and an attitude that could strip paint.

The woman had chosen the *wrong* damn house.

And it was all Liam's fault.

A cameraperson waved jauntily from the porch, but Aidan ignored him.

He got out of his truck. When he strapped on his tool belt, his scowl was so deep it actually hurt his jaw.

His brother came out onto the porch. "Hurry up!" Liam slapped at his watch. "You're twenty minutes late."

Who cared? Aidan sure didn't. "The Golden Spike was crowded."

"And you couldn't get your coffee to go just *once*."

Aidan shook his head. "I like to sit at the counter in the morning. You know that."

"I know you jawjack with the old guys like you're seventy."

"Is she here?"

"Tuesday?"

"Whatever the hell her dumb day-of-the-week name is."

Liam folded his arms over his fancy pinstriped shirt that probably cost a hell of lot more than Aidan's three-for-ten-dollars T-shirt had. "You sure woke up with your pants on cranky."

Cranky? Understatement of the century. Aidan was mad as hell. "Yeah?"

"Seriously, you have to keep that attitude off camera."

Aidan rested his hand on his favorite hammer as if he were a sheriff with his hand on his holster. "It'll make the show spicier, don't you think?"

"No, I think it'll make us look like a bunch of country-yokel jackasses."

"Whatever. Let's just get the filming over with."

Liam blocked Aidan from entering the house with his body. "I'm not kidding. Pull it together. I don't care how you feel about this house. It's hers now."

That was the whole goddamn problem. This house—this old, perfect, wonderful, gorgeous beast of a house—belonged to someone who wasn't Aidan. To a woman who was coming in from the outside. "I was going to buy it. You know I was."

Liam winced. "And I wanted you to. But your bid wasn't accepted."

"You could have made sure it was."

"You would have had to outbid her big time."

Aidan had only had enough in savings for a small down payment. If he'd sold his condo in time, he could have probably outbid her. "Yeah, well, I would have needed you to sell my condo for me."

Liam bristled. "*You* would have needed to make that decision about two months earlier."

"I'm supposed to know the future?"

"Besides, the seller chose *her*."

Aidan's jaw tightened. "The seller is LouAnn Callahan's ungrateful cousin who never even came to town to look at the place, and you're the broker. You should have pulled some strings. It was my dream." The words felt like gravel in his throat. He shouldn't have to say this to his brother. Liam *knew*.

"I know. Does it help that you still get to work on it?"

"Seriously?" An outsider would tell him what kind of crappy tiles she wanted. He'd have to build an in-house sauna or something else just as ridiculous for her. It would all happen on film, with the television cameras rolling. She'd be the customer and she'd have to be right. About everything. Then he and his brothers would hand over her key at the end of this episode of *On the Market*. He'd never have another chance at owning the place he'd loved since he was ten.

From the entryway, the cameraperson named Anna called, "Hey guys, the light is coming into the kitchen perfectly. Let's catch this."

"We're coming," Liam said over his shoulder. Then he said to Aidan, "Get a grip. I mean it."

9

Aidan rubbed a hand over his mouth. He tried on a half-smile, but it didn't fit his face.

Liam shook his head. "You look like you're about to chew off someone's leg."

"It's going to be yours, if you don't get out of my way."

Inside, it was chaos. The living room was full of light poles aimed toward the group standing in the dining room. Extension cords coiled over every inch of floor.

"Powder, sir?" A kid who couldn't have been more than nineteen tried to wave a brush in his face, but she ran away when Aidan scowled.

A complete stranger tugged at Aidan's T-shirt and adjusted his tool belt while another person stuck a mic pack into the back of Aidan's pants. "I feel violated," he said, but no one was paying the slightest bit of attention to him.

"Rolling," someone yelled.

Liam waved him into the kitchen. "Aidan, I want you to meet our client. This is Tuesday Willis."

The woman was medium height with a medium build. She had medium brown hair that was medium length and the medium brown eyes to match. She wore cat-eye black glasses that were probably in fashion but which really served to make her look like a librarian. There was nothing remarkable about her except the fact that she'd stolen Aidan's house right out from underneath him. She might have been tolerably pretty if Aidan hadn't despised her so much already. But hell, the more he hated her, the less chance she'd choose him to date during the renovation. If

Aidan did his job right, there was a one-hundred percent chance she would choose Jake as her on-screen date-night target.

She smiled.

Aidan didn't.

Her handshake was firm, but clammy.

Liam said, "Tuesday, this is my brother Aidan. He'll be the work foreman, the one in charge of the renovation. That's Jake over there."

Jake, the idiot, waved cheerfully. Yeah, he wasn't losing his dream today. Tuesday smiled back.

Liam went on, "I thought we could get a head start on what you might be thinking of doing with this place."

"Well, I—"

Aidan cut her off. "And what *is* that?" He could practically feel the camera zooming in on his face. Sixteen million people would watch him be a son of a bitch on television, but he didn't care.

"Sorry?"

"What is it that you want to do with this place, exactly-?"

Tuesday glanced at Liam. "Should we just jump into that?"

Liam nodded. "Sure. Why don't you walk us through a couple of rooms and tell us your vision for the place."

"Okay, then." With her forefinger, she pushed up her glasses. Her nails were painted, predictably, medium pink. "Well, I guess I was thinking—"

"What are you going to do with the wood?" Aidan thumped the frame of the door that led into the kitchen. It was old Doug fir, and while it was scratched and dinged, it was perfection itself.

"Um. Paint it? I was thinking yellow walls with white trim?" She looked up at the dark beams that soared overhead. "Wouldn't that be pretty?"

She'd just failed.

"No." Aidan brushed past her, ignoring the fact that her face had fallen. He led the way into the kitchen. "What about in here? What's your idea of fixing this up?"

Tuesday had rallied and was smiling at the camera. Obviously, they hadn't told her that she wasn't *supposed* to look at the cameras, that she was supposed to talk just to the other people as if there wasn't an entire crew hanging on their every word. "Well, I love this old sink."

She was right about that. A deep farmhouse ceramic sink, it was perfect, set deep and low in the old butcher-block countertops.

Aidan waited.

"But I was thinking of marble countertops. You know?"

There it was. No surprises here. Turning his dream home into a hipster Pinterest house was going to be the worst gig in the history of Aidan's construction career. "Let me guess. You're looking for more of an open plan."

She smiled, her face lighting up. Behind those glasses, her eyes sparkled. For one moment, Aidan felt the tiniest bit guilty about growling at her.

Then she said, "Exactly. If the dining room led into—"

"Yeah. I get it. Hang on." He stalked past the crew, out the living room, and to his truck. The cool, damp outside air was welcome against his heated face. He pulled out his biggest sledgehammer and stormed back inside, holding it like a baseball bat.

"Aidan." Liam's voice was a warning.

"No, I get it. I see our client's vision. I know how this is going to work. Let's get this show on the road."

Ignoring the roar in his own head, Aidan pulled on a pair of safety goggles. "You might want to stand back," he said to Tuesday.

"Wait, what?"

He swung the sledgehammer back with all the force of his body, slamming it through the wall that stood between the living room and dining room. Plaster rained down, the lathe behind it snapping like firewood. "There we go. A good start!"

Tuesday Willis stepped forward. She put one hand firmly on his chest, and with her other, took away his sledgehammer, hefting it as if it were a lightweight rubber mallet. She looked directly into his eyes, and Aidan felt a thud in his torso that he didn't see coming.

Enunciating clearly, Tuesday said, "That's a load-bearing wall, you *idiot*."

CHAPTER TWO

The only reason Tuesday Willis knew it was a load-bearing wall was because Liam Ballard, the realtor brother, had told her so when she'd asked if it could be taken out to make more room in the kitchen.

But it was a good thing to know, apparently. The brother who'd stormed in and punched a hole in that wall was going to be the one who had to fix it. Good thing she had his hammer now, though it was way heavier than it looked.

"Seriously?" Aidan, the stormy brother, looked at his other two brothers. The one who lived on a boat—Jake—was already leaning on the countertop, laughing so hard it looked like he might hurt himself.

Liam's jaw had fallen open, and he clutched at his tie. "Why did you *do* that?"

"The load-bearing wall is the south one."

Tuesday shook her head and patted the intact drywall above the hole. "The west one. You're telling me *he's* the foreman?" She saw a cameraman grin and felt the lens zooming in on her. "You can't tell load-bearing from non?" As if she could. Her heart pounded, and she clenched her fingers more tightly around the hammer's handle, willing the shaking to stop. She'd already been ten kinds of nervous—arguing with the foreman wasn't helping.

Aidan's scowl was so dark he was practically summoning clouds. Well, at least Tuesday was sure which brother she *wouldn't* be picking.

Felicia, the slim showrunner who looked like a model (no pressure or anything—the woman's legs went up to her armpits) threw her hands up in an I-surrender pose. "Okay! That was exciting! Good job, Aidan, not taking out an entire beam."

"Or bringing down the whole house." Jake grinned.

Felicia gestured to the side door. "We'll probably edit that a little bit, so don't worry about a thing. While the crew patches that up, let's all go out onto the back porch, shall we? Anna, can you bring out the lemonade and those green glasses?"

Cameras swiveled. The tall sound guy ducked both himself and his boom mic under the door.

Tuesday held out the sledgehammer, using every muscle in her arm to do so and determined not to show it. "This is yours, I think."

"Yeah." Aidan took it as if it weighed as much as a pencil. "I'll be needing that."

He turned, following his brothers and the camera crew.

On the porch, as workers set up lighting and tested things, Tuesday leaned on the rail. Her scar felt hot under her shirt, a sure sign of stress.

This was probably the dumbest thing she'd ever done in her life.

Back home in Minnesota, Tuesday's mother had gotten a lawyer friend to look over the contract. The lawyer said it was good, that both she and the network were protected by it. He'd said, "Careful, though, if you do sign it, you'll have to go through with it. They're serious, and they have the money to back that up."

That was okay. Since the settlement, she had the money, too. Tuesday had signed the contract, and in her memory the signature, instead of being in the black ink she'd used, was bright red, as if she signed in blood.

Tuesday leaned forward and inhaled.

This view was why she'd chosen this house over the other two. It was all a set-up, of course—she'd been surprised at how much of the reality show was done in advance. The network had sent her 360-degree videos of the interiors and exteriors of three houses. They said she could "choose" any of them and they'd start the buying process (with her money, of course). Even though she'd already chosen the older house on the bluff with the view down to the bay, she'd spent her first day in town on camera, pretending to have interest in the other two houses she hadn't bought. Felicia had explained it all to her. "You've seen my episode, you know I've been through this, and I agree, it's just weird. But you're a grade-school teacher, right? This is make-believe, that's all. Now, while looking at me, not the camera, tell me what you think about the last place." Talking to the camera while gazing at Felicia was hard. The woman made Tuesday feel even shorter and rounder than she was. By the time they were done with the show, Tuesday would probably resemble a beach ball just from comparison.

Liam, the realtor, had walked her through the other houses on camera. "You've got a good, big budget, though that much cash doesn't go as far here in California as it does in Minnesota. For your nine hundred thousand, we've got to purchase a house *and* get the construction done."

It hadn't been hard to look worried. "Can we do that?"

"Can we? Leave it to the Ballard Brothers!"

Today she'd not only explored the bluff house for the first time, but she'd also 'chosen' it, on camera. It had been a relief, getting to show her true excitement. The house sat at the end of a cul-de-sac. An old Victorian three-story house, it seemed to smile into the street with its the upper windows eyes and the faded red door the surprised mouth. It was pretty, but it looked old. It didn't seem to promise that much.

Through the house and into the back, though, that's where the magic was. Tuesday had been hopeful, looking at the video tours. She'd been *right*.

Then Aidan had shown up with a chip on his shoulder and a hammer to match.

Now the man was pacing in the garden below. It would have been easy to stare at his broad shoulders, but luckily there was the whole bay behind him to focus on, a brightly sparkling body of water. She would *not* gaze at the way the back of his jeans fit his rear end. Nope.

The wraparound porch was wobbly but it held their weight. Below the porch spread a small garden—mostly roses, two dark blue hydrangeas, and several enormous lavender plants. One low oak tree spread boughs that looked made for climbing up and hiding under. A long hedge ran along the bottom of the garden, and beyond that, the earth dropped away. From the porch, she could see the tops of the buildings on Main Street. And over those dark roofs, the bay.

The Pacific.

Finally, she was here.

"Look!" Tuesday pointed. Brightly colored scraps of fabric hung and swooped over the water, too far away to make out more. "Are those really hang gliders?"

Liam answered her. "Yeah. It's a popular hobby here. Aidan does it a lot. Have you ever gone hang gliding?"

"No! No way."

"Nothing like it. We should get him to take you up."

"No, thanks. I'm not that tall, and I like to be close to the ground in case I need to hit the deck."

"It's not that scary. And the thermals in the area mean you can stay up a lot longer than you can in other places."

A shiver ran through. *Stay up.* No, thanks.

She glanced down into the garden again, motion catching her eye.

It wasn't Aidan—he was just coming back up onto the porch.

There. Where the bottom of the garden met the neighbor's fence, a small gate moved.

It cracked open. Just an inch.

Tuesday held her breath.

The wooden gate parted enough for a small head to poke into the garden.

A girl.

She had long dirty brown hair that tangled past her shoulders. She was thin, dressed in a blue dress and black tights. Even from this distance, Tuesday could tell the girl had huge eyes that were currently scanning the yard as if she were looking for something specific.

Tuesday glanced at the camera crew, wondering if anyone else was noticing the apparition. If the girl hadn't been wearing gigantic orange tennis shoes, she would have wondered if she were a garden sprite, or a wraith only visible in her own imagination.

The girl caught sight of Tuesday.

When she saw that Tuesday had noticed her, she jumped like a startled rabbit and pulled the gate shut silently. She was gone.

Tuesday turned back to the conversation which had gone on swirling around her. "Who lives next door?"

Felicia looked up from her clipboard distractedly. "Mr. Hildeboom. He doesn't get out much, but he's a good nosy neighbor. He's already called the cops on us twice, thinking we were breaking in."

"No." Tuesday pointed. "Down there."

"Huh. I don't know. Anna, did you get releases from that neighbor?"

Anna tugged back her headset so the earphone came off her ear. "Yeah. Um. Woman and daughter." She put the headset back on and said something into it.

Felicia shrugged. "Sorry I don't know more."

It was okay. It was a little early to try to get chummy with anyone.

From behind her, Aidan said, "That's Ella."

Tuesday turned. "Who is she?"

"Well, for her age, she's a good power forward."

Tuesday raised her eyebrows.

"I coach basketball." He sounded grudging, like he hated even telling her that much.

"Ahh."

Felicia was back. "Okay, we need you over here now, Tuesday. Time to answer some questions.

It was so managed.

So prescribed.

She'd known a lot of reality TV was staged, sure, but she'd never taken the time to imagine how many other people were involved. For every person on the porch—her, Felicia, the three brothers—there were another two people. Each of them had their own camera- and sound-person. Below their feet, the porch groaned.

"Is this safe?" Tuesday couldn't help asking it. "Would it be better to film in the garden?"

It was as if no one heard her. They all kept testing, chattering about things that didn't make sense to her.

Okay, almost no one.

Aidan, that sour look still on his face, said, "Stand where the nails are. There are beams below those. Or there should be."

His words were probably meant to be reassuring, but the way he barked it made Tuesday's stomach flip with anxiousness.

"Nah, it's fine," said Liam. "I've been walking all over it for the last two weeks."

"Okay." Good. She moved to stand on the edge of the porch and leaned over the rail. The air smelled amazing— there was something sharp in it, maybe pine, and something crisp, like the leading edge of rain. Clouds amassed in the sky over the water, and the air was heavy with moisture. She'd thought California was the desert and palm trees and cactus, but this wasn't dry—this was verdant. She smelled ozone and salt, and the grin that had landed on her face when she'd first seen the house crept back.

Behind her, Felicia said, "So Tuesday, what do you think of it out here?"

Tuesday turned and smiled, somehow surprised by the camera lens that was focused on her. It made her shy again. "It's gorgeous. I love this porch." She stamped her foot lightly. "I love how it's a little shaky. A little old."

"A lot old," said Aidan grumpily. He shoved a lock of dark brown hair out of his blue eyes. Handsome, yes. But pricklier than the cactus she'd been expecting.

She didn't care, though. Under her foot, the porch boards groaned. "Hear that? That's the sound of a house coming back to life. How long was it empty, again?"

"Might want to stand on some nails." Aidan pointed.

"Seven years," said Liam.

She didn't need to stand on nails. This house already loved her back. "It'll hold me, she said. "I can feel it."

The timber creaked happily.

Then it complained even louder as her foot went through the wood.

CHAPTER THREE

Before Tuesday really understood what was happening, Aidan lurched forward, putting his hands to her waist, gripping her almost painfully.

"What the *hell?*" All she knew was that she was falling sideways. Was this what an earthquake felt like? She was thrown off-balance, or she would have been, had Aidan not effectively moved her two steps backward. He jumped sideways to avoid going through the porch, too, releasing her waist as he did so.

"Oh." Tuesday smoothed down her black shirt. To avoid falling over when he'd grabbed her, she'd instinctively grasped his upper arm. The muscles in it had been *roped*. Knotted. She tried to find her breath. "Oh."

"You're *welcome*." Aidan's voice was a tiny bit less gruff. "You okay?"

"Fine." The hole her foot had punched in the porch was at least six inches wide. "I guess you were right about where to stand." *He* was the one who smelled amazing, not the air. The scent of pine was coming from him, as if he'd bathed in wood chips. For a disconcerting second, she wanted to bury her face in the front of his soft, blue shirt.

"Did you get that on camera?" Felicia asked a camera person.

Tuesday shook her head hard. "God, I hope not. I must have looked ridiculous."

Aidan nodded. "We both did."

Felicia smiled. "America loves ridiculous. Makes them feel at home."

Well, America was going to feel very at home, then, because Tuesday was currently feeling preposterous.

"More importantly," Felicia continued, "Are you okay?"

Tuesday nodded. "I'm fine."

Felicia snapped her fingers and got the hole covered with a board by a guy wearing a network TV shirt. Tuesday felt more embarrassed than ever, her cheeks painfully flushed. She'd gone *through* the porch.

Felicia didn't seem to mind, though. She pointed. "Okay, we're ready to roll. Tuesday, I'll place you right here, yes, that's perfect. Ballard brothers, line up there, along the rail. Good."

Tuesday wondered desperately what her face was doing. She pulled her shoulder blades toward each other and felt the scar on her stomach stretch.

"Not so much sticking out of the boobs, okay?" Felicia made a fluttery gesture in front of her chest.

Blushing harder, Tuesday glanced at Aidan.

Yeah, his eyes were right there. On the breasts she'd been thrusting in an attempt to gain a half inch of height.

"Sorry." She shrunk into herself again. "Sorry."

"No worries at all. Okay, we'll do this as many times as it takes, and it's no big deal if we all flub up. No stress here. And...we're rolling."

No stress, we're rolling. Those two things did *not* go together.

"Tuesday!" Felicia's voice was suddenly so bright it sparkled like the blue water of the bay below. "Now that you've chosen your house, the only other thing left to choose is the Ballard brother you'll date while they're renovating your house. Do you have any thoughts about the men so far?"

Tuesday's heart raced. She looked at Liam, who'd been so kind to her throughout the whole emailing of the last six weeks. But he was paired off with Felicia, from the very first episode.

"Yeah, he's off limits, I'm afraid." Felicia grinned, and it appeared to be real, reaching her eyes. "Liam's no longer on the market. But these other two fine Ballard specimens are. Aidan, head honcho of the Ballard construction crew."

Aidan rolled his eyes, crossed his arms, and leaned against the door frame.

"And seafaring Jake, jack of all trades, master of quite a few of the same."

Jake smiled cheerfully. "Hey, Tuesday."

Not Liam.

Not Aidan.

It was easy. "I'll date Jake."

Jake stuck an elbow into Aidan's side, earning him a glare.

"Great! Can you tell us why?"

"Well." Tuesday hesitated. "I guess I'm just going by how they look."

Felicia grinned. "Tell us more. Be honest."

Honesty? Okay, then. She was good at that. "Jake is smiling." As she said it, Jake's smile got bigger. "He looks sweet and nice. When he met me for the first time this morning, he gave me a hug. He looks like he'd be kind to puppies and help old ladies across streets."

Aidan snorted and rolled his eyes again.

Tuesday continued, "And Aidan there kind of looks like an angry horse."

"Excuse me?" Aidan straightened.

Adrenaline shot through Tuesday's fingertips. "Well, no. If you were blowing steam through your nose, you'd actually look more like an angry bull in cartoons."

Jake hooted. "Oh, yeah. Paw the ground, Aidan."

Aidan glared. "Are we done here?"

"What the hell is your problem?" Tuesday couldn't stop the words, nor did she want to. No matter how she looked when it was played back, no matter how rounded her shoulders or boring her expression was, she didn't want to be someone she wasn't.

"What the hell is yours?"

"*I'm* not the one acting like a bully here."

"*A bully?*"

A shiver scampered down Tuesday's spine but she held her ground. "Yep."

"You're the bully here."

"What?"

"You come into town and—"

"I was invited." By the network, true, but it had still been an invitation.

"Okay, back it up further, then. You apply to be on this show—"

"My mom applied for me."

Aidan appeared to be about to say something else, but he stopped. He wore a button-down denim shirt and dark blue jeans. A tool belt was strapped around his waist, and it looked like it had been right there, on those hips, for years. His jaw was sturdy, and he had a tiny cleft in his chin, something neither of his two brothers had.

Tuesday would think he was the hottest Ballard Brother if he wasn't such a gigantic dick.

"Your mom," he finally said.

She tilted her head. "Would you like to say something about my mother?"

Jake shook his head and muttered, "Don't do it, dude."

Aidan didn't listen to his little brother, apparently. "Your mommy applied you for the show?"

Heat rose to her cheeks. "She heard about it before I did." True, her mother had told her several times about the show, urging her to apply, and Tuesday had ignored her.

"Let me guess. You lived near her?"

She raised her chin. "Down the street." This would be the first time she'd ever been farther from her parents than when she'd been in college in Minneapolis, ten years before.

"So what you're saying is that she was trying to get rid of you?"

Tuesday sucked in a breath. It wasn't true.

Of course, it *was* what she'd thought at first.

Are you trying to get me out of here? To leave the state and you and Dad? Tuesday had been teasing, but there had been a small, serious part of herself, too.

Her mother had shaken her head. *You've wanted to live in California as long as you've known where it was.*

Palm trees. Sun, year round. Avocados. Surfers.

But I wasn't really serious.

Her mother's eyes had been, though. *The twins will be in your class next year. Are you ready for that?*

Of course, she wasn't.

Of course, she'd accepted when the network's offer had come through. She hadn't thought October would be fall-like in California, but it was. Red and orange blazed the trees. At the downtown café, Tuesday had heard people exulting in the early October rain. She hadn't seen a single palm tree except for a sick-looking one outside the airport four hours south in San Francisco.

Aidan was still waiting for her answer. On camera, she supposed it would be more interesting if she told him off. But she didn't need to. "Yep, she was just trying to get rid of me, I totally admit it. What's your mom like, Aidan?"

His eyes got wide, as if she'd just kicked him below the belt. Without saying another word, he spun on his heel and pushed his way through camera equipment to jump off the far side of the deck.

"Hey!" Liam shouted. "We still need to film you talking about the interior plans."

A single middle finger was the response.

Tuesday's heart was pounding, a little too hard. "I'm sorry. I guess that was my fault."

"Are you kidding?" Jake shot her a thumb's up. "That was great. Can you do it again later?"

CHAPTER FOUR

Aidan used his key to let himself into the Ballard office—it felt less weird than it used to. Liam and his adopted son Timbo used to live above the office, but they'd recently moved in to Felicia's remodeled tree house, and the space still felt empty. The old house sighed around him, and the floorboards creaked. He flipped on the desk light, preferring that to advertising to all who drove by (his brothers) that someone was inside.

Of course, Liam had told Aidan to make a copy of the contract he'd signed.

And of course, Aidan hadn't done it.

Liam was the oldest, the paper pusher. He'd practically been born with a stack of Post-its in his hand. He hoarded pens like other men collected dirty magazines.

Jake, the youngest, was the devil-may-care brother. He'd never met a pretty girl he couldn't fall for or a boat he didn't want to sail.

Aidan was just the tool guy.

And sometimes? Just a tool.

It wasn't that he felt *bad*, per se, about the way he'd treated Tuesday Willis. She'd deserved it. *No, she hadn't.* The small voice in his head sounded a lot like his stepfather Bill's.

Aidan just wanted to see how long he was committed to this job. They hadn't shot his reactions yet, but he knew the plans they'd made. Open-plan kitchen. Redo both bathrooms. Turn the two small bedrooms on the third attic floor into one bright, skylit loft. New porch.

Here it was. The contract had the network's name on the top in red, and each page was thick and watermarked.

Aidan flipped the pages quickly. He found the page detailing the cancelation clauses. "Yeah. Well, that's a shit sandwich, all right."

The light flipped on, and the room went bright. Liam stood in the door frame. "I like ham and cheese better. But you and I have always had very different taste."

Aidan threw the contract onto the desk. "I'm stuck doing it?"

"What are you talking about? You're the head of construction."

"I have a crew. They're good."

"*On The Market* is about *us*. The brothers."

"She chose Jake. You don't need me in this episode at all."

"Jake can barely saw straight."

"I'm going to give him the next project to head, you know that."

"Okay. But not on camera. You're forgetting that this is supposed to be advertising. Not only are we doing this to make the money to open Ballard Youth, but we're also getting to the point where we can pick and choose our clients. Remember when we were barely making it? That wasn't very long ago. Everything's changed now, and it's due to the show."

Aidan folded his lips.

"Scotch?" His brother pointed to the kitchen.

"Hell, yeah."

While Liam poured two shots, neat, Aidan opened the back door. He stood in the dark under the overhang as it began to drizzle again. "Thanks."

Liam stood next to him. "Sometimes I think we should sell this place. Rent an office on Main."

"But it's ours." Theirs, together. The three men had bought the falling-down place together after their stepfather Bill Ballard had died. They'd fixed it up together, stage by stage. Each of them had spent time living in it, most recently Liam and his son.

"I know."

"Hey, this house is the only retirement plan I have."

Liam nodded in the darkness. "Sleepy beach town like this? It might not be the best plan in the world. And what about your condo?"

"The one I should have sold, you mean? Do you really want to go there?" Aidan tried to shrug the tension out of his shoulders. Instead, he got a bonus neck cramp.

"Anyway, you know better than any of us about the property value zooming upward."

"True. You don't really want to get out of doing this show, do you?"

"Do you think I can?" Hope rose in Aidan's chest.

"No way in hell."

"Goddamnit."

"Seriously, what is your problem, man? It can't be just the old Callahan house. I know you wanted it, but I was pretty sure you'd get over that."

Never. "That house was supposed to be mine." His to fill.

"Whatever. Get over it. Is it about the girl?"

Fine. Let his brother think that. "I don't like her."

"What's not to like? She seems nice. That's like not liking soup."

"I don't like soup, either." It was true. Soup was boring and didn't fill a man up.

"Shoot, I forgot that." Liam looked at him. "I know you wanted that house. And I'm sorry as hell you didn't get it, you know I am. Want to tell me why you wanted it so bad, though? I feel like I'm missing a huge piece of the puzzle."

"Bay view."

"Nope, that's not it."

Aidan tried again. "That wraparound porch."

"The one falling through?"

"The one I would have fixed."

"You mean the one you *will* fix."

Aidan shot back the rest of the scotch, liking the heat as it burned down his throat. He could do with a couple more of them. Maybe he'd hit the Golden Spike saloon on his way home.

See if there wasn't a woman inside who could distract him.

The plain face of Tuesday Willis rose in his mind. Round cheeks. Mousy hair. Little to no makeup even though a makeup person had kept hovering over her. Pointless, really. She looked like the schoolteacher she was in those glasses. Makeup wouldn't change that.

"It's not because of the fact you used to eat dinner there sometimes with that teacher, Mrs... what was her name? That was a million years ago. That can't be it."

"That's not it," he lied.

Aidan shook his head. The meals he'd had in that old dining room had often just been chicken and sweet potatoes. Meatloaf. The family he'd shared the meal with was normal. Kind.

It hadn't been a big deal, now that he looked back at those nights as a grown-ass man.

But the Callahan house had been his dream, and now it wasn't.

"Fine," said Liam. "Keep it to yourself, then."

"Yep."

In the dimness, Aidan could barely see his brother's expression, but he could *feel* it.

It felt way too much like pity.

CHAPTER FIVE

The room at the bed and breakfast was dim, even when Tuesday switched on all the lights. She counted six of them, all with twee pink shades, and none of them more than twenty watts, apparently.

At least the WiFi was strong enough to run Skype.

She sat at the small rolltop desk which didn't actually roll closed—it was fake like so many other things in the inn—and perched her laptop on a pile of books she'd brought with her. "Mom?"

"Hello?"

"Can you see me?"

"Honey?" The image over her mother's photo continued to spin. "I can see you. Can you see me?"

"Click the camera icon."

"I don't know where that is. Ron? Help me!"

Tuesday blew out a breath. "It's blue. It's right under me on your screen." She pointed downward, toward her right knee. "See it?"

"Oh! There it is."

The screen went blank as her mother disconnected.

"Come on, Mom." Tuesday made the call again.

"Honey! I pushed the button you told me to. Can you see me now?" Her mother pushed at her brown bob. "I don't know why you have to look at me, anyway. Can't I just look at you?"

"You look pretty, Mama."

"Oh." Margo Willis smiled. "Should I put on lipstick?"

"No way. You look great." In the background, Tuesday heard her father say exactly the same thing. *No way. You look great.*

"You, too." Her mother's nose became huge as she leaned toward her camera. "Let me look at you."

"I've only been gone two days."

"It's been forever."

Tuesday took a deep breath, as if she were trying to inhale her mother's gardenia perfume from here, more than two thousand miles away. "Is it snowing yet?"

Her father, invisible in the background, yelled, "Ninety-two today!"

Tuesday had left in the middle of the October heat wave, sure that as soon as she did, an early storm would blow through and break her heart. "I already miss snow."

Her mother's nose got closer. "You know, if we can have this weather, maybe you can have snow there sometime."

Sometime.

That meant a while.

I want to come home.

She didn't say it.

She didn't even really mean it.

But the thought was there.

"How's it going there, Mom?"

"Me?" Margo sat back in her chair, her hands pressed to her heart. "Us? There is *nothing* to report."

Her father yelled, "I got the Studebaker running for thirteen seconds—"

"Nothing at *all*. We want to know about you. Have you seen the house?"

"I did."

"Was it at all like the video they sent you?"

In the background her father shouted again, "Because if it wasn't, we'll sue!"

Both Tuesday and her mother sighed. Ron Willis had never brought a lawsuit against a single person, even though he loved to yell about it. He cheerfully threatened to sue the mayor for parking in the wrong spot, and the local grocer for running out of avocados. When Tuesday had been awarded her settlement, there had been no one more surprised than her father. *Well, I'll be damned. Something good came out of all that. See what I mean about suing?*

"The house was better than the video."

"You're kidding!"

"I felt it when I opened the door." Even though four different cameras at different angles had been trained on her, even though every word she'd spoken was being recorded, she hadn't been able to stop the involuntary words from leaving her mouth: *I'm home*. "But I don't know. Am I just letting myself get carried away?"

"Yes. Exactly." Her mother nodded. "That's just what you should do. Tell me more."

"The top floor is going to be remade into one big bedroom, with a skylight. The kitchen is going to be opened up. We'll need a new porch, because the old one is rotten. I—um—I kind of stuck my foot through it."

"Are you okay?"

"Yeah. And I heard a producer talking to the brothers about something may be wrong with the foundation."

"*The foundation?*" her father roared.

"I think it's cracked a little? Or needs shoring or something." Or both. She'd read it in the reports, and she'd seen the line where it said what it would cost to fix. It had been a large number but no one seemed to be concerned about it.

A crease dug into her mother's brow. "You signed all the papers?"

"Done deal. I own a house, foundation and all."

"Well." Her mother brightened. "Anything can be fixed."

That was what her mother always said.

It was too bad it wasn't true.

"What if I can't find a job here?" Tuesday hadn't done her research, not thoroughly enough. She should have made calls to the school district offices. She should have found out what attrition they were expecting, if they had current openings. But beyond a cursory internet search, she hadn't. The school year had already started, after all. It wasn't ideal timing.

She'd just packed six boxes of essentials and moved.

She'd *moved*.

Her heart rate picked up again. It kept doing that, and she was starting to find it annoying.

"Honey. Take a breath."

"You always say that. It would be literally impossible for me to forget to breathe, you know that."

"Just do it for me. Take a bigger one."

Tuesday did. It didn't help.

"You'll find a job, honey."

It was nice to hear, even if she didn't quite believe it. "Okay."

"And even if it takes a while, that's all right. You've got enough money."

Blood money. That was all it was. Tuesday hated the size of her bank account, while at the same time she marveled at it.

Her mother put her mouth to the camera again, as if she thought that was where the microphone was. "You said you could think of this as your gap year. Your sabbatical. Isn't that a lovely idea? You can work on your new house and read all the books you haven't had time for. Who gets that lucky, right?"

Lucky.

It made her want to laugh, but if she did, she might cry, so instead Tuesday nodded. "You're right. But, Mama, it's so far from you." She couldn't remember the last time she'd called her mother that. Years, maybe a decade or two.

Her mother spread her fingers and wiggled them. "Oh! I almost forgot! What about the brother?"

Could she fake an internet connection going out? Hang up on her mother and text her that she'd talk to her later in the week?

That wouldn't be kind, though.

"I met the brothers."

"Which one did you choose?"

"The boat guy."

"The youngest?"

"Jake. Yeah."

Her mother pulled back, looking up at the ceiling. "Hmmm."

"What?"

"I didn't think you'd go for him."

"What do you mean? Did we watch the same shows together?"

There were only five episodes so far. One the inaugural show, Liam and Felicia had fallen for each other, which took Liam out of play. It was suddenly a show about the other two brothers. Aidan had been chosen twice, as had Jake. They'd seemed to be having a great time, and at the end of each show, the woman in question would cheerfully say something like, "I've found the home of my heart, but I'm still looking for the right guy. These Ballard brothers are great, but they're still on the market."

"No," said her mother. "We watched the same shows. I just assumed you'd go for the middle brother."

"In my classrooms, the middle siblings are always the ones you want to watch out for."

"Pish."

From what sounded like another room, her father yelled, *"I don't trust that big guy, the one named Aidan!"*

"Thanks, Dad! Neither do I."

Margo said, "But Aidan's so handsome. All wide chin and big hands and long legs. And those deep blue eyes."

"Mom!"

"Don't forget you're my woman!"

Tuesday's mother giggled in delight. "Have fun with the young one then, my love. He's a sweetie, too. Keep us posted. Now, the oven just dinged. Love you." With a kiss pressed to the camera, she was gone.

He's a sweetie.

Tuesday closed the computer. Her mother thought she knew the men in *On the Market* because she'd seen five shows. But Tuesday was here, and she knew not one thing about the men or the town or even what she herself was really doing here.

She'd run away from everything she'd ever known, from the people she loved, because she felt such unalleviated guilt. She lifted the hem of her shirt and traced the long, rippled scar.

Maybe here she'd be able to throw the guilt into the ocean, where it could float out and join the island of trash that sat in the middle of the Pacific Ocean.

CHAPTER SIX

A s Aidan pushed his way into the Golden Spike Café, he suspected he hadn't had enough caffeine yet to deal with getting coffee with his brothers. Sure, he'd had three cups at home, but it still wasn't enough. They were having a business meeting, and they should have had it at the office, but both of his brothers were completely addicted to Molly Darling's plum muffins.

The café was crowded, of course, but his brothers had saved the corner of the counter for him. Great. He'd have to sit with his back to the diner, one brother on either side. At least he'd be the closest person to the coffeepot under the counter.

"You look like shit." Jake pushed him a clean, empty coffee mug.

"Thanks." Aidan rubbed his jaw. He'd missed a big spot shaving. That would be a good look later. Patchy as a pirate, with the mood to match. "Where's Nikki?"

Liam pointed. "Dealing with those ten tourists that just came in. They're asking for extra hot skim lattes with caramel salted baby-tear foam."

"That'll go well." Nikki was obviously stuck. Good thing Aidan's arm was long. He stood and leaned all the way over the counter and grabbed one of the full coffee pots. He was careful to not go all the way behind the counter. Nikki got sensitive about that. As long as he just reached, he was okay. He served himself and topped up his brothers' cups, too.

"Hey!" Norma, one of the town drunks and one of Aidan's favorite people, waved at him from the next table. Her collection of necklaces tinkled and her muumuu was exactly the same color red as the tablecloths, so that it looked as if she were wearing the table. "Hit me!"

Aidan poured coffee into her mug. "You're out of cream." He took the silver jug and swapped it for a full one from the tiny fridge next to the coffee pots.

"Here you go."

Norma looked up at him. She was normally all smiles, but this morning, her lined face was wary. "I don't like it."

"The coffee?" He sniffed the pot. "I'm just pouring it. I didn't make it."

"No. Something's not right." Norma clutched her necklaces, jingling them. "I don't know what it is. But something's off."

"Earthquake weather, maybe?" It was what locals said to explain anything that didn't feel right. They were always wrong, except for Norma. She always knew when one was coming.

"Nah." She flapped her hands. "Something else. Someone's coming to town."

"You sound like a carnival fortune teller in a movie." He smiled. "Now I'm expecting to look out and see clowns coming after us with butcher knives."

She looked affronted, her dark eyebrows climbing her forehead as if they wanted to run up into her short gray hair. "I love clowns. I don't understand where all this recent clown hatred is coming from." She shut her eyes. "I'm going to sit here and think happy clown thoughts now."

Aidan put back the coffee pot and slid in to his seat.

"Happy clown thoughts," whispered Liam.

Jake guffawed.

"Speaking of clowns." Liam jabbed his fork over Aidan's coffee cup at Jake. "Where are you taking Ms. Willis on your first date?"

That was dumb. Why would his brother already be concerned about that, when they hadn't even started work on the house yet? "He's got time."

"The network really wants us to move on this."

Jake's eyes widened. "I don't know. I did surfing with that one gal, and bungee jumping with the other one. I'm kind of out of ideas."

"Such a romantic."

"Hey," Jake said. "I live on a boat. I don't need romantic. When's the boat's a-rockin'..."

"Classy," said Aidan. "You gonna say that on air?"

"Hell, no." Jake fiddled with an invisible bow tie. "I like to look good on camera. Not like you morons."

Nikki, the hostess and sometimes-waitress, appeared. "Hey, guys. Aidan, thanks for helping with the coffee round."

"Do I get a tip?"

She retied her apron. "Here's one. Stay out of Molly's way today. The oysters weren't delivered and the mayor has some fancy shindig here tonight."

Aidan sensed an opportunity. "Can I help? I can run down to Tomales Bay if you need me to."

"No." Liam elbowed him. "We need you on site today, you idiot."

"Can't need me that much."

"*You* are the one who's got to figure out how to jack up the foundation and fix it within the week."

Aidan forgot about the oysters. "That's completely impossible."

"They're paying us to *make* it possible."

Nikki sighed. "Thanks, anyway, Aidan. I think she'll make the sheriff do the run, and I'm going to try like hell to send her, too. She needs to get away from this place for a few hours." She nodded at someone at the register and moved away.

Damn. Aidan could have done with a trip out of town. He and his brothers had lived in Darling Bay most of their lives, first with their parents, and later, with the man their mother married, Bill Ballard. Bill had loved them with a ferocity neither parent ever had, and it was because of him that they'd all grown up healthy. Their father had been addicted to meth. Their mother had been addicted to opiates and inappropriate men—except for Bill.

Bill had loved them.

And he'd loved Darling Bay. There wasn't a much better combination, if you asked Aidan.

It didn't mean that sometimes a man just needed to leave town at a high rate of speed and not look in the rearview for a few days.

"No," said Liam.

"What?" Heat crept up Aidan's neck.

"You've got your running face on."

"Exercise. Please. My job gives me all the exercise I need." Aidan was being deliberately obtuse. Liam knew him too well, that was all. "There's something about her. I'm just not feeling this job."

"Bullshit."

Aidan jumped. Liam almost never swore.

"This is just about you being selfish and wanting that house for yourself. You can't have it. You lost that round. Now be a man and get the hell over it."

Be a man. "Are you saying I'm *not* one?"

Jake leaned forward. "Hey, dudes. Calm down. It's not a big deal."

Not a big deal? The Callahan place was, literally, the house of his dreams. The one he'd always planned on buying the second it was for sale, even if he had to sell his bodily organs to make the cash needed for the down payment. Then it had gone on the market, and because of the TV show, he'd lost it. To a rich out-of-towner who was made richer by the bonus the network paid—they made the down payment to sweeten the deal. Not that she seemed to need it, of course.

Rich girls, man. You could have them. "It's a big deal to me." That was all he'd say about it.

"Just get her to sell to you when the show's over," Jake said.

That was it. "*I just need to get her to sell to me.*"

Jake was reaching for the plate Molly was setting down. He wasn't listening. "Thanks, Mol."

"You don't get all of them. Share with your brothers. Six muffins. Three of you. Do the math."

"You're the best, Molly. Thanks," said Liam.

Aidan sat in stunned silence.

"What?" Jake pushed the plate closer to him. "You don't want yours?"

Aidan blinked. "Whoa."

Liam reached across. "I'll take his."

Aidan strong-armed the plum muffin out of Liam's grasp. It crumbled a bit, but he got the majority of it. He repeated himself. "I just need to get her to sell to me!"

Jake rolled his eyes. Around a big bite, he said, "I justsh shed that."

"That doesn't seem like a good idea." Liam was always the cautious one. That's why he handled the finances.

Aidan said, "It's a *great* idea."

"How do you think you'll go about doing that?"

"She just needs to hate living here."

Liam and Jake both frowned.

Aidan, though, smiled. Maybe this could work.

A commotion rose outside the front windows of the café. As if he'd summoned her (had he, perhaps? had Norma?) Tuesday walked past, trailing cameras.

"Speak of the devil." Aidan stood. He ignored his brothers' protestations. "I believe I'll go see how's she's enjoying her time in town."

CHAPTER SEVEN

D arling Bay was so quaint that it almost made Tuesday wonder if the whole was a mafia-run front. What town could possibly be this sweet? The café they'd just passed, the Golden Spike, reminded her of Luke's Café in the Gilmore Girls. It appeared to be connected to a saloon of the same name across the parking lot, a building so old-western looking that she expected a posse to come riding up to the doors, desperate for cool whiskey and warm women.

Just a bit beyond the café, a gazebo nestled in a pocket park. The white wood of the building was surrounded by low pink roses, and white tulle hung from its beams, as if a wedding had just ended. Tuesday looked at her feet—sure enough, grains of rice were embedded in between the paving stones. "Did someone get married here?"

Felicia Turbinado said, "Oh, yeah. There's a wedding a week here, sometimes more. It used to be a popular place for locals to get married but since the show, a ton of tourists are taking up the tradition. Last spring, during El

Niño, it rained so much that this little park became a rice paddy."

"Literally?"

Felicia nodded. "White rice shouldn't have sprouted, but someone brought organic brown rice, and it did. We had rice growing right here on the coast. They cut it down, of course, and resodded the grass, but I've always thought that was a shame. I bet the rice grown from it would be so sweet from all that wedding love, it could probably cure a disease or two."

"Well, that's a delicious flight of fancy, ain't it?"

The voice came from behind them. Tuesday knew who it was before she even turned around.

Aidan stood tall, his boots spread on the sidewalk like he'd earned the right to fill the space.

"Aidan!" Felicia stood on tiptoe to kiss his cheek. Right, she was kind of a sister-in-law. She looked *happy* to see him.

Tuesday wasn't happy to see him. She was *something* but she couldn't quite name it, and she didn't like things she couldn't name. They made her nervous.

"Where's the handsome brother?" Felicia asked.

"Obviously." Aidan stuck a thumb into his chest. "I'm right here."

"No, the *really* good looking one."

"Oh, that one. He's in the café."

"Plum muffins."

"It's hard to resist their call."

He hadn't acknowledged Tuesday at all. He looked at the camera crew, and nodded to the guys holding the mics. He smiled widely at an older woman who walked right through middle of the rather impressive traffic jam they were creating on the sidewalk.

But he hadn't looked Tuesday in the eye once.

It irked her. "Hi, Aidan."

He appeared to jump. "Oh, hey. I didn't notice you."

Jackass. His jibe worked, though. Tuesday immediately felt drab in her black knit dress that had seemed professional when she'd put it on that morning.

"Hey there." She pushed up her glasses with one finger and tried to meet his gaze directly, but he'd already looked away.

Felicia pulled a small notebook out of her pocket and flipped a couple of pages. "Since you're here, can we get a walk and talk with you?"

Wait. What? With Aidan? "I thought this stuff was all planned out in advance."

"It is. By me." Nothing seemed to flap Felicia. What would *that* feel like?

"Yeah, okay." Aidan pushed at his hair. "I look all right?"

"You're putting the reality back into reality TV. You look fine," said Felicia. "The wind would destroy anything we did with your hair, anyway."

Like it mattered. Men. The makeup person had spent thirty minutes on Tuesday that morning, and she still felt disheveled. She'd worn a dress for the first time since she'd last been in a classroom, but it was a wool-nylon knit. She'd thought it had been going to rain again but thirty minutes ago, the clouds had evaporated into nothing. Was that what fog did? The mugginess had stayed, though. Sweat trickled down the base of her spine into the back of her underwear. She felt sodden. They had fog in Duluth (they'd once had a fog horn in the harbor) but she'd heard that ocean fog was different. This was. She knew her hair, which went frizzy on a good day, was probably triple the size it had been when she'd last looked in a mirror.

Aidan, though?

Damn.

He wore a dark green T-shirt that read "I'll get my tool kit" over the image of a roll of duct tape. His jeans were old, light blue in most places. A dark blue patch had been sewn on near the knee, and it didn't look like the pre-distressed jeans that came from the store. Who loved him enough to sew on a patch for him? A girlfriend? Not his mother—it had come up a couple of times on the show that they'd been raised by their mother's second husband, Bill. She shouldn't have jibed him about it the day before. But he'd needled her so hard she hadn't been able to help it.

Network people hooked up Aidan's mic pack, sticking it into the back of his jeans. For a moment, Tuesday wanted to be the one with the excuse to touch him. His face managed to look rugged and grumpy at the same time, his jaw stubbled and his brows drawn close. "Ow! Do y'all really have to be so far into my pants?"

Into his pants. Tuesday's brain flashed white, as if snow-blinded by a freak Minnesota blizzard.

"We're walking." Felicia pointed forward. "And we're talking. We'll flash back to this as if you just got to town, Tuesday. Can you act like you're seeing it for the first time?"

That was easy. It felt as if she were. Darling Bay lived up to its name, but at the same time, it appeared real. A guy on a bike whirred past, his bell dinging cheerfully. A father led a crying toddler toward a car. A woman wearing a lot of makeup, twin slashes of color at her cheeks, didn't look up from her cell phone and almost walked straight into Gene, one of the camera operators.

Felicia poked Aidan in the arm. "So Aidan, you're a long-term resident as well as the head of construction in *On the Market*. I'm sure Tuesday would like a quick tour. Do you mind?"

Aidan nodded. "You bet, Felicia. This town really means a lot to me, and I'd love to show you a little bit of it, Tuesday." He pointed down a small alley. "You mind if we detour down here?"

Tuesday didn't trust his tone of voice, but she trooped on, trying to forget that one of the cameras never left her face. She plastered on a half-smile and hoped it didn't look too much like a grimace.

"Down here, yeah, follow me." Aidan half-knelt and gestured into a drain at the edge of the street. "You see that?"

Everyone looked at Tuesday, and she realized, belatedly, that she was the star of the show.

Oh, crap.

"The grate? Yes."

"This right here was the starting point of the Great Rat Standoff of 2006."

Definitely not what she'd thought he was going to lead with. "Oh?"

"As far as we can tell, Ira Higgins, who was five at the time, released his sister's two rats here. He'd read that they liked to be in fields and wanted them to be free. But they were Norway rats, and though we didn't know it at the time, they're larger and hardier than any of the other rats we had living under the town."

Tuesday frowned. "Okay?"

"Within six months, rats had taken over the town."

Felicia laughed melodically. "Oh, Aidan."

He stood. There wasn't a glimmer of humor in his face. "That was a rainy year, you might remember, one of the wettest on record. And as you might guess, the water table underground is pretty high, since we're so close to sea level. In certain parts of town, we're actually below it." His voice lowered as if he were telling a ghost story. "And every time it rained, rats came crawling out of every toilet in town."

Tuesday jumped backward, as if rats were pouring out the grate toward her. She bumped into Felicia, and then skittered sideways, trying to regain her balance. "No, they didn't."

"They did." Aidan nodded solemnly. "I have to admit, I never saw one come up my own toilet—"

"Ah-ha!"

"But I did hear a noise in my bathroom trash can."

Tuesday swallowed her shiver. "A rat?"

"A mama rat. With nine tiny little rat babies."

Oh, God. Tuesday did *not* like rats. At home they'd stayed in the barn, where rats were supposed stay. "You're making that up."

He held up his palm. "Scout's honor."

Felicia inserted herself between them. "All right, how about show us something else. Something nice."

"Nice? Okay. Follow me!" Aidan wove his way through the group and led them out of the alley and across Main Street.

Damn, he had a great ass. His jeans looked just right. Tuesday felt her whole face heat. Could the camera tell where she was looking? She aimed her gaze over his left shoulder and kept walking.

Good. They appeared to be headed for the beach. Another block, and she was certain. "Careful crossing the street here," Aidan called over his shoulder. "Two pedestrians have been hit right in this spot."

Doubtful, Tuesday looked around. "There's, like, no traffic."

"Not the time of day for it."

She followed the direction of his pointing finger to the clock tower that sat on top of a short, square building. Just after nine. "If now isn't, when is?"

"School time. All those mothers picking up their kids from school. The whole town slows almost to a crawl. It's like a Bay Area traffic jam, right at two-forty. You would *not* believe what it's like."

He was right. She didn't. "I don't drive." *Anymore.*

He looked quizzical, his eyebrows drawing together briefly, but then he said, "Okay!" He stuck his hands in his front pockets and rocked back on his heels. He turned to face the ocean. "Can you guess what we're looking at here?"

Tuesday looked at the water. Waves thundered against the beach, pounding with a force she could feel in the balls of her feet. Gulls circled overhead, calling loudly down to them. The air smelled clean, as if the color blue had a scent. "The Pacific Ocean?" She tried to make it sound funny. Cheeky. Instead, it came out like she actually wasn't that sure.

"Correct! But that's not the only answer. Anyone else?" Aidan didn't give them much of a chance before he answered his own question. "This is also the most treacherous stretch of coastline on the Northern Coast. Any guesses as to the number of people drowned out here in the last century?"

Tuesday shook her head. She was pretty sure Aidan was working hard to rattle her, so she kept her mouth shut.

"I'll tell you then. Two hundred and fifty-seven."

"Holy—"

"And the majority of those are in the last fifty years, since surfing caught on."

"That's awful." Why was he telling them this? Was he trying to scare her for some reason? "But I don't surf, so I should be okay."

"We've had six tourists swept off Bald Cypress Rock by rogue waves."

Tuesday squinted at him. What was he playing at? "Did they live?"

He shrugged, slowly. "Who knows? Their bodies were never found, if that's what you're asking. Some could argue they washed up somewhere else and were fine, but I think we would have heard about it."

"Is this the haunted tour of Darling Bay?"

Aidan appeared to brighten. "No. But it should be! Follow me, we'll go look at Miss Bridget's old boarding house. It's been closed up for years, but on nights with no moon, you can hear moaning from the garden."

"Cats having sex?" Tuesday guessed.

"Maybe." He frowned her direction. "But maybe not. Who can tell?"

"I'm pretty sure I could tell the difference between feral cats mating and a ghost, but maybe that's not a common talent." Tuesday temper was getting frayed. What was the point of this?

A dog walker leading six or seven dogs of all sizes approached. At the same time, a mother with a baby in a snuggly on her chest caught up behind them. She led a toddler by each hand.

Tuesday smiled at her. "Three of them? Your hands are full."

The mother looked exhausted, but she smiled back. "Yep."

"Everyone, let's move out of the way over to the left here," said Felicia to the camera crew.

Aidan stood next to Tuesday, so close she could smell the aftershave he'd used—pine and mint and something else like mulled cider, maybe. "That's a lot of dogs," he commented.

"And a lot of kids." Tuesday froze in place so that she didn't accidentally touch him.

A screech went up from one of the toddlers, as if he was startled by one of the dogs.

In response, a tall reddish dog barked sharply in the child's face. A black and white dog skittered sideways, pulling its leash out long.

The mother, distracted by the barking and the shriek, didn't notice the leash. She caught her ankle and tripped.

Tuesday held her breath. Jesus, the baby on the woman's chest—

But the woman hit the sidewalk on her shoulder, shielding the baby from the fall with both her arms.

Confusion reigned. Dogs barked, the baby set up a howl, and every person on the camera crew rushed forward to help the woman up.

Tuesday felt ice-bound in place next to Aidan.

The toddlers, suddenly released from holding the woman's hands, raced away from the dogs, all of whom were straining to sniff at them. Both children shot into the street.

Without stopping to think, Tuesday hurled herself after one of them. She felt, rather than saw, Aidan do the same.

She scooped up the child closest to her and threw him onto her hip. Then she jumped back to the curb, her heart lodged somewhere in her throat. The child in her arms screamed blue murder, as if he'd been hit and thrown by a passing car.

Tuesday gasped a breath. Aidan was next to her, the other child sitting on his hip.

There was still no traffic. The danger had been minimal. It had just been a gut reaction. She'd imagined mortal danger when it hadn't existed.

The dog walker had raced down the sidewalk, apologizing over her shoulder, probably trying to get out of the melee. The mother stood, her leg scraped, but the baby didn't appear to be much bothered by the tumble. "Oh, God, thank you. Thank you!"

Tuesday met Aidan's eyes.

He looked amazing with a baby on his hip.

Totally, completely *not* acceptable.

CHAPTER EIGHT

S he looked amazing with a baby on her hip.

Oh, man.

That wasn't the thing that Aidan needed flashing through his mind right now.

Focus.

He set the toddler on his feet and led him back to the mother. "No problem. Automatic. Sorry. Hope I didn't scare the guy."

Tuesday relinquished her kid to the mother who said she was fine, reassuring the dog walker it wasn't her fault. Felicia said something about walking toward the property. Fine, whatever. As long as he didn't have to think about Tuesday and the way she'd lunged, without looking, into the street after the kids.

The way he had.

The way he would have done had there been a truck barreling down the silent road.

She would have, too. He knew it.

The Callahan house wasn't far, less than four blocks away and up the small rise, but it was a long enough walk for Aidan to bring his heart rate down.

His idea to scare her away from town was stupid. It wouldn't work—he'd been dumb to think it might have. She was too brave for that.

What he needed to do was get her to hate the house itself, just enough so that by the end of construction, she'd want to sell it just to get rid of it.

But he had no bright idea how to do that. He fell back, using the excuse of asking Gene a question about camera stability. When Gene answered him, he forgot to listen.

He was too focused on watching the way Tuesday walked. She had short legs. Nothing like Felicia's, who was walking next to her. Felicia walked gracefully, like a cat in a jungle.

Tuesday walked with shorter strides, purposefully, as if she were holding down the ground as she trod over it. Her legs were pistons, accurate and energetic.

How could short legs be that sexy? She was in a black dress that reminded him of an old school uniform. It looked scratchy. It didn't fit her well, hanging loose at her waist, and tight at her hip. It didn't give her the sexy-student look, but he didn't think that was what she'd being going for. On the contrary, the skirt gave her the look of a grad student too busy studying to bother with the way she looked, the look of a woman who didn't much care what other people thought.

It was an ugly, unsexy dress.

Damn, it made her legs look amazing in comparison. Had he ever watched such strong calves move before?

"You shoot?"

Gene was still talking to him, and Aidan hadn't heard but the last two. "What, like with a gun?"

Gene looked confused. "What? No. Are you a photographer?"

"Oh, no, I don't. I can barely figure out where the camera app is on my phone." He did his best to pay attention to the conversation but there they were, right in front of him: Tuesday's incredibly shapely, powerful calves.

Finally, they reached the Callahan house. Felicia asked if he had any stories about it. "Maybe not like the town stories, though. What about a nice tale or two?"

"Sure." Aidan didn't feel very sure about anything, actually. He led them into the living room, where the view looked down to the beach they'd just walked from. "You know the wood of the house is Douglas fir, right? This was built in 1905, and it's built on bedrock. They say that when the great quake hit San Francisco in 1906, the top level of the house slid right off."

Tuesday frowned. "But that's four hours south. They felt it up here?"

"Of course. That's just a hop skip and a jump when it comes to how earthquakes ripple through this state."

"What was the top level?"

"It was more like an upper deck, and the builders hadn't finished attaching it to the roof properly. It was a widow's walk. Do you know what that is?"

She nodded. "Where women watched and waited for their sailor husbands to come home."

"Romantic, right?"

Tuesday looked startled. "Very."

"Well. Not this house. When Mrs. Callahan first built it, she'd already lost her husband. Legend says he'd been an alcoholic and he'd beaten both her and her daughters. She wanted the widow's walk on top so that she could keep an eye on her property, to make sure she kept men away."

"Why?"

"She didn't want to marry again. She'd inherited his fortune, and she wasn't interested in losing any part of it. And she wanted her two daughters to remain spinsters."

Tuesday's eyes sparkled. She had that curious superpower of making him feel like he was the only person in the room when she looked at him like that. "That's wonderful."

He'd thought it was terrible when he'd heard the story, so many years ago now. Mrs. Brown, his third grade teacher, had told him the tale, when he was sitting right here, in this room. Mrs. Brown had seemed to like her husband quite a lot—at least, she kissed him when he came home for dinner as if she did. But young Aidan had wondered how many other women worked hard to keep men out of their lives.

What if...? he'd asked Mrs. Brown.

What if what?

What if she'd been meant to fall in love with someone else?

Mrs. Brown had smiled her special, sweet smile at him, the smile that made him feel smart, like he could finally learn the eight times-table. *You're a romantic, huh?*

I think that people are meant for each other. That's what his mother always said. That's why she kept leaving Bill and going back to their father, over and over again. *Do you think that?*

Mrs. Brown had looked at Mr. Brown across the table. *I do.*

What if the widow had another person who'd been meant for her but she kept him away?

We'll never know, will we?

Tuesday went to the window to look down into the garden and over the top of the town. "Just think of her. Alone with her daughters, taking care of them. The world might shake the top of their house off, but it can't shake them apart. They stayed together, as a family, all the women in one spot."

"Until each of her daughters eloped."

The corners of her mouth turned down. "Oh."

"Sorry to disappoint."

"Is it *true* the whole top of the house came off?"

Yeah, well. It was possible that Mrs. Callahan's builders just hadn't finished securing the widow's walk to the roof when the quake hit. Construction blamed a lot of things on the quake that year. That made more sense to Aidan than having the top part of a house slide off, which it wouldn't have done, unless it hadn't really been there to begin with. "You're the kind of person who likes to know things for sure, huh?"

Tuesday crossed her arms, and in those black cat-eye glasses, she looked like a stern librarian. "Yes. I do."

A *hot* stern librarian.

Yeah, he didn't need to think about her like that.

"We'll never know. Okay." Aidan patted the wall. "She's still built sturdy, though. Even the cracked foundation we can fix pretty quickly with enough manpower. We need to talk about what you want to do to this place."

With a little wheedling, hopefully he could talk her into doing as little damage to the old place as possible. Heck, maybe it would turn out that this was a blessing in disguise. She'd fork over the money to fix the place up so that when he bought it from her, he'd have less to do.

If she left in a rush, he might get a truly good deal.

Time to put his mind to it.

CHAPTER NINE

Tuesday had more than a week of downtime, as the crew got the necessary supplies and manpower on site. *Labor,* she corrected herself. Just because Aidan Ballard was sexist didn't mean she had to be. (She had noticed women on the site, though, so at least they weren't sexist in their hiring.)

Jake was busy on site, too, and Felicia had told Tuesday to just enjoy the relaxation of nothing to do. "No dates, no working, just spend time getting to know your new town. Jake's planning your first outing, which will be next Friday night, so that's all you have to think about. Let me know if you need suggestions of things to do. There's a good local spa about fifteen miles north, if that's what you're into, or I can tell you where the outlet mall is."

Tuesday didn't like shopping much, unless it was for books or fancy cheese, and she didn't love strangers kneading her body, either. "Is there a bookstore in town?"

Felicia wrinkled her nose. "No. Sadly, our only bookstore closed about six years ago. But the library is great, and you can get a card. Just use the Callahan address."

The week had passed more quickly than she thought it would, though. The library gave her a card, and she read two thrillers. She stopped by the house three times to see what was happening. Each time Aidan either ignored her or glared in her direction. The south side of the house was jacked up with a machine that looked like it could lift a skyscraper, and workers moved around underneath.

What if it fell? Cars slipped off jacks, didn't they?

It made Tuesday too nervous. She wouldn't go back until that part was done.

Then it was date night.

She wasn't nervous, exactly. It was what it was—a means to an end. The show revolved around the brothers fixing up the house, and the buyer dating one of them. Because she was playing along, the network was making the whole down payment for her. It was a good reason. Her mother had been smart to sign her up for the show.

And Tuesday didn't mind going out with Jake. He seemed kind and funny the few times she'd spoken to him.

But she felt unsettled.

The person she'd really be nervous to go out with would be Aidan.

So thank goodness that was off the table. As she dressed for the date, she kept her mind firmly *off* the middle Ballard brother. She didn't think about Aidan's roughened, wide hands once. She most certainly didn't think about the way he'd smiled at the mother of the toddler he'd grabbed. Or the way his eyes had twinkled. Nope. She would *not* think about that.

Tuesday focused on knotting the tie of her red wrap dress. *Jaunty.* That's what her mother had said, when she'd given it to her. Just make a jaunty bow at your hip. *Let me show you how. Oh, just look at you. Cute as heck, sugar.*

That was fine for her mother to say. Her mother could take a paper sack and some string and wrap a present that looked as if it had been professionally done. Tuesday, on the other hand, bought gift bags to put presents in. As soon as Scotch tape got involved, things went sideways on her.

Packaging herself into the dress was the same kind of challenge. No matter what she did with the tie, it didn't seem to fit her well. She honestly couldn't tell if the dress was too large or just right. When she draped the panels between her breasts, the place the fabric met in the middle seemed awfully low. So much cleavage. Was that something that looked better or worse on screen? She couldn't make a decent-looking bow to save her life, and just opted for an overhand knot.

Fine.

She looked just fine.

That wasn't bad, was it? That she kind of looked boring?

She added black heels and silver drop earrings.

She put on lipstick, the kind that didn't wear off. Her mother had bought her this, too. It wasn't until Tuesday poked her head outside and checked her makeup in the natural light on the balcony that she realized the lipstick was *red*-red. Red-light district red. Did her mother want her to look like a street-walking floozy on national television? Tuesday rubbed at it with a tissue, but the stay-on property was strong, and the tissue came away clean.

The curling iron was heated, and she took a stab at curling the ends of her hair, but whatever curl she got into her locks almost immediately fell out.

She stopped trying. She pointed at herself in the mirror. "You are plainly plain." It hurt, even coming from herself. "Plain."

To her parents, plain was sturdy. It was strong. Something to be proud of. Her father made plain wooden furniture in the garage on his days off. Her mother wore a plain gray apron when she cooked. Frills were for other people, not for them. Even the lipstick her mother chose had probably been picked because of its long-lasting quality.

For just one moment, Tuesday closed her eyes and wished she were someone else.

Someone pretty enough to make men gasp as she walked past.

She imagined, just for a split second, Aidan seeing her as a vixen. Aidan losing his breath.

Nope. Jake was the one who was picking her up, and Jake was the one she should be imagining.

As if she'd called for him, he knocked on her door.

"Hey," he said. From behind him in the hallway of the Cat's Claw, the camera waited, Jake's silent followers. Behind *them* stood Pearl Hawthorne. She wore an extra layer of lipstick, Tuesday noticed, though Pearl's was more orange.

Pearl bobbed up and down, gripping the neckline of her sweater. "Will I be in this scene? Me? When will I be able to see it. Will you send me the footage?"

"You look great, Tuesday." Jake seemed to be sincere—his smile wide. He kissed her chastely on the cheek and said, "Shall we?"

Tuesday wished they didn't have to.

The restaurant he'd chosen, Caprese, was nice. It was a touristy place, with red candles and a view of the boats in the marina.

"I like to eat here because I can see my house." Jake pointed to a pier where four boats were docked.

"Which one is it?"

"The green one."

"Ah. Pretty." She hoped it was the right thing to say about a boat.

"Do you like being on the water?"

"Mmmm." A camera person took a step closer and zoomed in on her hands. She stopped fiddling with the napkin. She was anxious somehow, but not about Jake, exactly.

"Yes? No?"

"I get seasick."

"Oh." Jake's eyes dropped, and he poked at the tablecloth with a finger. Then he glanced up hopefully. "How seasick?"

"Kill-me-now sick." Guilt washed over her. "I can't even stand on a dock, usually. Once I ate at a restaurant that was perched on stilts in Lake Superior. I got seasick there, and it wasn't even really moving. Just the idea that the pier might rock a little set me off. I'm sorry. I bet it was gorgeous out there, sleeping at night." She imagined being next to Jake on a creaking boat, being in his bed. She imagined hurling into a bag while sitting on the side of the same bed.

Yeah, that wasn't going to happen. Her skin felt like it didn't fit, and the chair was uncomfortable beneath her.

Jake took a quick sip of his wine. "Not your fault, is it? You can't help it."

She couldn't. But she wished for a moment she could.

Dinner passed slower than any dinner she'd ever had anywhere, including the four course meals her gran used to make on Easter. She limited herself to one glass of wine, which seemed like a prudent idea when in front of multiple cameras.

They made awkward small talk. Whatever Jake said seemed to circle back to boats, and every time he brought them up, he seemed embarrassed and concerned, as if just talking about them might make her queasy. "Sorry. Where have you sailed—I mean, where have you traveled recently? Besides Darling Bay."

Tuesday ignored the question. "What's the plan for the rest of the night?" She couldn't handle much more of this. It was agony, and they were both in it, obviously. Maybe he'd kiss her later—maybe she'd be startled by chemistry flaring between them.

But probably not.

Jake's face fell again. "I was going to show you around my boat."

Tuesday grimaced. "I'm sorry."

"It's okay."

"No, I really am sorry." She tried to paste brightness onto her face and shove it into her voice. "What else is there to do in Darling Bay on a Friday night? There have to be some fun things to do, right?"

He blinked. "There's the Golden Spike saloon."

"What else?" It was the bar the Darling Songbirds owned, and it seemed like a place the whole town might congregate, and she didn't know if she was ready for that.

"There's night fishing in the estuary but..."

"Boat."

"Yeah," he said sadly. "And there's drinking on the ferry out to Sandbar but..."

"Ferry."

"Yeah."

She'd add this later to the never-ending, never-sent email to Diana. *It was the worst date ever. And it's going to be televised. The only thing not horrible about it is that Jake is sweet and the bread is delicious.* "Does the saloon have a pool table?"

Jake's eyes lit a tiny bit. "Yeah. You play?"

Tuesday raised her palms and let them drop. "Well, I've been called a shark, but I'll only admit that to you." And the millions of people who would see her on TV.

Millions.

Her stomach dropped away. This was the worst idea ever.

"I'm game if you are," he said, standing.

Anna, the woman who seemed to run things when Felicia wasn't around, said, "What's the noise level like in there? Will we be able to film?"

Jake grinned. "It's quiet as a library."

CHAPTER TEN

J ake tried to hold Tuesday's hand as they walked toward the bar. She thought it was a fine idea. Holding hands. Nothing more romantically filmable except a kiss, right? And sure enough, the camera crew fell behind them and filmed their backs as they walked.

But it felt weird.

Holding hands with Jake reminded her of something. It took a minute to figure out what it was, but then she had it—when she was little, she loved to swing from her father's hand as they walked. That's what it felt like.

Like holding Dad's hand.

As smoothly as she could, she pulled her hand back and said, "Just have to get something in my purse." She checked her lipstick as they'd left the restaurant (the red still clung to her lips—it would probably still be on at her funeral), so she couldn't really do that again. She had to do *something*, so she pulled out a pen and clicked it once before dropping it back in her bag.

Jake looked at her, but thankfully he didn't ask. He stuck his hand back into his pocket and ambled along next to her.

As they entered the bar, Tuesday found that Jake had lied about the noise level, and God bless him for doing it. He must have been having as miserable a time at the quiet restaurant as she had.

A four-man band played on the small stage—a sign said they were Dust & Rusty. They weren't bad as country music went, and several couples danced up close to the stage. The saloon itself seemed pretty full. Jake pointed to a small table that had just opened and pointed. "Want to grab that one? What would you like?"

"A beer. Any kind." She wasn't picky. Just something to give her hands something to do while they waited for the pool table to open.

"You got it."

Before she sat, she approached the pool table tucked into the far corner. A beer lamp swung gently above it, as if someone had just touched it with a cue stick on accident.

"How much to play?" she asked the man with his back to her who was about to take a shot. "Can I call a game?"

The man pulled his stick back smoothly and shot the seven ball into the corner pocket. "Fifty cents. Put your quarters on the rail. You can play winner." He turned.

Aidan.

Tuesday felt heat shoot to the top of her head. He stood stock-still in front of her, tall and handsome and utterly distracting. A lock of his brown hair had flopped over one eye as he leaned to take his shot, and now he pushed it back.

Of course he was here. Her heart raced, but she pulled two quarters out of her purse and lined them up carefully along the pool table's edge. "Cool."

He nodded without smiling and moved to take his next shot.

Tuesday took the chair Jake had pointed out. She held her purse on her knees.

She felt like an *idiot*, and she had no idea why.

This was a date. A date that she'd agreed to be on. So her date's brother was here. Why wouldn't he be? It was Friday night in a small town—most likely half the town would cycle through here tonight, right?

The camera crew, meanwhile, was earning stares.

Anna placed her camera on the table and crouched next to her. "I'm concerned with the noise level. We've shot in here before, but never on a crowded night."

She said something else that Tuesday couldn't hear. "What?"

"I said, we can get some video, even with the low light, but I don't think we're going to be able to get audio."

"Is that a problem?" Tuesday didn't want to leave. Not anymore.

Anna shrugged. "It's not ideal. But if you do some large visual cues, that'll be enough for background later."

"Visual cues?"

"You know." Anna looked at the bar like she wanted a beer, too. "Lean against Jake. Smile up at him. Laugh at his jokes, touch his arm. That kind of thing."

She meant *Fake it.*

Tuesday glanced at Aidan. He was talking to his pool partner, leaning close and speaking directly into her ear. The woman, a brunette with high cleavage packed into a tight white shirt, gave a happy laugh and flung her arms around his neck. She pressed her breasts into his chest and planted a kiss on him that Tuesday could almost hear from fifteen feet away.

Yeah, Tuesday could fake it. That wouldn't be a problem. "Sure."

CHAPTER ELEVEN

While Aidan kind of hated asking Clois to do him thefavor, she was definitely getting into the role. *Hey, I need you to pretend to be my girlfriend. Okay?* She hadn't even asked why, which was a good thing, because he didn't have a great answer. She'd just thrown herself at his chest and kissed him. She tasted like candy corn and smelled like roses, and combined, that was just too sweet for his tastes.

But at least she was enthusiastic, and she knew it was just a game.

God, he hoped she believed that.

Jake brought beers to the table where Tuesday sat. She looked...

He didn't know how she looked.

She looked like herself. She wasn't lighting up the bar, not the way Clois did next to him, nor the way Adele Darling did while pulling drinks. Tuesday wore a simple red dress that showed off the rack he hadn't known she had. She wore red lipstick that didn't really seem to suit her coloring. Her black heels seemed too high for her, and she wobbled a bit while she walked.

She was normal.

Regular.

Kind of plain.

And he couldn't tear his eyes off her. There was just *something* about the woman that was driving him crazy, and Aidan hated that he couldn't name exactly what it was. She wasn't gorgeous, not even a little.

But she was completely mesmerizing.

It seemed rude as hell of her.

Aidan had been letting Clois win, because she was pretty adorable when she thought she was good at pool (she wasn't), but he had to nip that in the bud. Winner played the next person, and that would be either Jake or Tuesday. On his next turn, he ran the table, clearing his balls and sinking the eight right where he called it.

He whooped as both Jake and Tuesday stared. Clois laughed and kissed him again, this time with tongue. She was a sexy woman. He knew that.

He wished he cared, even a little bit.

"Who's next for an ass-whuppin'?" Aidan smiled as wide as he could pull his face.

Jake looked at Tuesday. "Want to go?"

She shook her head. "Go ahead. I'll play winner."

Jake grinned. "Then you'll be playing me, darlin'. My brother ain't got nothing on my pool-playing prowess."

Like hell. Jake *was* usually better than Aidan, but not tonight.

While they played, Clois sat with Tuesday. That made him nervous. And helpfully, the nerves made his shots better. Within fifteen minutes, he'd wiped the floor with Jake, who'd only sunk one ball.

The women approached.

"You suck." His brother scowled. "You can't let me impress a girl?"

"Depends on who you wanted to impress." Aidan held out his arm, and Clois pressed herself against his side, smooching him loudly on the cheek. He could almost feel the hot pink of her freshly reapplied lipstick burning into his skin.

"This beautiful lady." Jake held out his arm in the same way. Tuesday leaned awkwardly toward him and then away, fiddling with the bow of her dress at her side.

Huh.

That was something. Did they have any chemistry at all?

He shook his arm as Clois tried to shimmy closer. "So. Tuesday. You're playing winner, right?"

She inclined her head. "Jake, do you mind?"

"Heck, no. I might buy us both another beer, though. My pride is wounded and I'm hoping more hops will help."

"Buy me one?" asked Clois, abandoning her role immediately.

"You bet," said Jake. "Kill him, Tuesday."

She took her time picking a cue stick, rolling it on the top of the table, checking each one for balance. Satisfied with a short one, she chalked it carefully. She hadn't really met his eyes yet.

That bothered him.

"So. You're a shark?"

She blew on the tip and rechalked as if her life depended on it. "Nah. I won two games in a row in college. That's about the best I ever was."

He'd go easy on her. He might even let her win. That would be the polite thing to do, after all. Tuesday and Jake were on the date. They should get to play pool together.

But he hated the idea of them playing together. "Rack or break?"

"Break," she said without hesitation.

CHAPTER TWELVE

Okay, so she'd lied a little bit. Not to Jake—when she'd told him she was good at pool, she'd meant it. She might have downplayed her skill to Aidan, though.

She'd won two games in a row back in college, yes, and she'd done it a thousand times. The local watering hole had been next door to her apartment, and the bar had been owned by her landlord. He'd gotten a kick out of her taking so much money off men trying to prove themselves that he'd lowered her rent on the condition she come in and play every Saturday night. He made good money the more men lost to her and moved on to drown their sorrows.

She could be polite and go easy on Aidan. Not humiliate the poor guy in front of his date.

She glanced at Jake and Clois as she set up to break. Clois was eyeing them back, her eyes greedy on Aidan.

Or Tuesday could let him have it.

She pulled back her arm and let her stick sail solidly into the one ball. It was a perfect break, sinking two solids.

"Nice." His voice was grudging.

She lifted one shoulder. "Luck."

He eyed her then. One eyebrow went up as his gaze went firmly down her body to her shoes and back up again. Tuesday blushed to her roots. "Hmm. I don't know if I'm buying what you're selling."

"Stick around." Tuesday sunk another solid, the five ball. "I might be persuaded to give you a discount." She moved to set herself up at the cue ball, expecting him to move out of her way.

He didn't. He held his ground.

He wasn't technically blocking either her or her shot.

But he was less than twelve inches away from her.

Too close.

"I'm coming for you, don't worry." His voice was a rumble next to her, pitched so that only she could hear him.

A shiver shot down her spine, and she tried to prevent her shoulders from shaking with it. She pressed her lips firmly together and leaned over, sticking her rear end out perhaps just a couple of inches farther than she actually needed to. That used to help in college—men got flustered the more she bent over. She sneaked a look up at his face.

It wasn't working on him.

He still had that one eyebrow raised, as if just waiting for her to miss her shot.

She scratched. "Damn it."

He laughed, and a bubble of unexpected happiness wound its way up her throat. Tuesday wanted to hear him laugh like that some more—that laugh was sexy as hell.

Tuesday might be in trouble. And not in the pool game.

"Step back, little lady."

She squeaked with fake outrage. She moved so that she was across the table from him. Just as he lined up his shot, she leaned forward, putting her cleavage on full display.

"What are you doing?"

"Sorry." She wasn't sorry. "Just checking out how you line up your balls."

His face got red, and she wanted so badly to laugh. She *was* being a little rude to Jake, she knew, but when she looked over at him, he was talking intently to Clois. Neither of the two were paying them any attention.

When Aidan glanced at her, she cocked her hip.

He sunk a ball with a clacking smack. "There!"

"That was my ball."

"Shit."

A camera swung her direction.

Oh, yeah. Tuesday wasn't here to play pool with Aidan. She was on a date with Jake. This was, basically, her only job right now, and she was screwing it up. She sunk two more balls in a row before missing the next one.

He hit three of his into the pockets. He'd looked at Clois and Jake, too, and he was more solemn now, too.

It was less fun now.

But it was just as intense. She was careful not to bend too low or laugh right up at Aidan, but when she moved around the table and passed in front of him , she could feel his heat behind her. He didn't get out of her way. She didn't want him to. At one point, the back of her dress brushed the front of his pants, and she desperately wanted to lean backward into him.

To feel him grow hard against her.

To hear him make a frustrated noise into her hair.

To peel herself away and throw him an impertinent smile before winning the game.

Instead, she just sunk the eight ball with a satisfying thunk.

Aidan's eyes narrowed. "You were probably born a shark."

"Fin and all."

"You swam before you walked."

"I did."

He reached to shake her hand. He was a good sport. "Good game."

She took his hand and regretted it, immediately.

His grip was warm and strong, his palms thickly callused. But he didn't let go when he should have. He held her hand two seconds too long, and they were two seconds she'd never recover from. Tuesday lost her breath, and a split second later, she lost her gaze in his dark blue eyes. He said something to her, something so erotic she almost lost her balance completely.

She couldn't actually *hear* what he'd said, though, over the pounding of her heart. "Sorry, what?"

"I just said I was going to get a beer. Do you want one?"

"No. No, thanks. I'm fine." She pulled her hand back and wiped both her suddenly-sweating palms on her dress. "I'm fine."

He slanted another look at her, this one completely cryptic, then strode through the crowd and away.

"Finally!" Jake stood at her side. "My turn. I predict you'll win, but then again, winner buys the next round, so I'm okay with that."

"Great." Tuesday smiled the best she could. She'd play him, yes, but there'd be no next round.

She was already drunk on the one beer she'd had. She was drunk on something else, too, something she didn't dare name, even to herself.

Jake turned out to be a good pool player. Then again, she didn't try to distract him the same way. He was solidly reliable when it came to bank shots, and he was better than she was at cross table shots.

While he lined up his next shot, Tuesday glanced at the table, but Aidan and Clois weren't there.

God, had they left?

Why on *earth* would she be bothered by that? She was being ridiculous.

That didn't stop her gaze from searching the room, though. Had they left together?

No, there they were. Aidan held Clois tight on the dance floor. Clois's arms were wrapped around his neck, and her cheek rested on his shoulder. Her expression was blissful.

"Your shot." Jake followed her gaze. "That's a weird match."

"Yeah?" Tuesday tried to keep her voice neutral. "Why do you say that?"

"She's asked him out a couple of times, and he's always said that she wasn't his type."

What is his type? She wouldn't ask though she longed to. "Well, they look happy enough now."

"Sure do. Clois is a hoot. They're bound to have a wild time together. Good for Aidan. He's been pretty alone for a while now."

Tuesday's jaw ached from clenching it. She forced her eyes back to the pool table. If she lined up the six and ten and sank both, she'd have a clear shot at the eight ball, and winning. Then she could go back to the Cat's Claw and take three aspirin for the headache that was starting right behind her eyes.

Smack. Both balls sunk.

"Nice!"

"Thanks." She pointed with her cue. "Corner, banked."

"You've got this."

Jake was so *sweet*. She looked up to smile at him before she took her shot. Twenty feet behind him, her gaze locked with Aidan's, instead.

He looked at her—into her. His expression was unreadable, but she could feel the heat between them, even at that distance.

Clois nuzzled her head into his shoulder.

But Aidan looked at Tuesday like she was the one in his arms.

Her core heated. He was making her wet. Just with that look.

And that was upsetting as hell.

Jake turned his head, probably to see what she was looking at.

Tuesday dropped her head and made the shot. Her sweaty fingers slipped at the last moment, and the cue ball shot up into the air.

It flew over the table at a high rate of speed, as if she'd thrown it.

Then it beaned Jake in the temple.

With a thud, he went down.

CHAPTER THIRTEEN

Aidan's first reaction was to laugh. No matter what, it was funny to see his brother clocked in the head. It couldn't *not* be funny.

But Jake fell to the ground, all the way unconscious.

Holy *shit*. He pulled away from Clois in alarm and dialed 911 from his cell as he raced to his brother.

Station One was less than four blocks away, and the crew were on scene almost instantly. By then Jake was awake. Barely.

"Hey." Aidan handed his brother a glass of water.

"This doeshn't taste like beer."

"Oh, my God, I've killed him." Tuesday kneeled next to both of them. "He's slurring. He's going to die. It's all my fault. It's *always* my fault."

Aidan's throat was tight. "He's been hit harder than that before by falling beams and my fast pitch baseball." But Aiden didn't like the slurring, either. It freaked him the fuck out.

The fire captain Tox Ellis said, "Jake should be evaluated at the hospital."

Aidan nodded.

"But I'm on a date." Jake pointed at Tuesday. "With her. Don't cry, Tuesday."

"Did he just call her Tuesday?" Tox made a note on his clipboard.

Aidan stood. "That's her name."

"Oh." Tox scratched out what he'd written.

Aidan touched the metal of the stretcher. "Can I come in the ambulance?"

"Me, too?" Tuesday leaped to standing.

"Nope. You can follow us, though. You two okay to drive?"

"I don't have a car here," said Tuesday. It wasn't what she'd said last week, that she didn't drive at all.

"I'm fine to drive—I'll take you." Damn it, Aidan didn't want her in his truck.

And God, he *so* wanted her in his truck.

The drive was short and almost completely quiet. Tuesday kept her hands interlaced and tucked underneath her chin, as if she were praying. She gazed out the side window, and when he asked if she was okay, she didn't answer.

It was as if she couldn't hear him at all.

"Here we go," he started as he turned off the vehicle, but she was already out of the truck and running for the doors of the ER.

Seemed like he'd misread the attraction between her and his brother.

That made him a gigantic tool. Had he really been flirting with his brother's date?

Aidan stared out into the dark parking lot. That was a new low, for sure. He scrubbed his face with his hands, then he followed Tuesday inside.

The Darling Bay hospital was small but professionally staffed. Aidan had spent more than his fair share of time in this emergency department. He'd crashed a motorcycle at nineteen and broken his left pinky and his collarbone. He'd fallen off a roof at twenty-one, breaking his leg. When he'd gotten his first Irwin 15-inch saw at twenty-five, he'd cut his thumb down to the bone. His older brother Liam tended to stay safe (not much danger in pencil-pushing) but Jake had had about the same number of emergency-room runs over the last fifteen years.

Julie, one of the ER doctors, was the one with Jake in room five. "Hey, Aidan."

"How's my little brother?"

Jake was sitting up on the paper-covered bed, pressing an ice bag to his temple. "I'll never play piano again, they say."

Next to him, Tuesday jumped. "What?"

Jake laughed. "I've never played. That joke *never* gets old."

"Trust me." Aidan shook his head. "It does."

"I'm so sorry," said Tuesday. The words came out of her mouth quickly, as if she was used to saying them. Sure enough, she said it again. "I'm so sorry. So sorry. So very sorry."

Jake waved a hand in front of his face. "Hey, Julie, will I be permanently disfigured?"

"From this?" Julie waited a beat. "No, not from this, anyway."

Aidan stepped closer and lifted the ice bag. "That's a softball-sized goose egg you got there. Is he concussed?"

"No sign of it," said Julie. "He's not slurring anymore, his vision is fine, and he's not nauseated. I want one of you—" She arched a brow at both Tuesday and Aiden "—to stay with him tonight. Make sure he's rousable and that no other symptoms pop up. Bring him back in if he gets disoriented or starts to throw up. But he's going to be fine." A siren sounded, tinny in the distance. "I'll be back when I can. Jake, I want you to stay for at least another hour, just for observation because of that loss of consciousness. Don't go anywhere." She ducked through the curtain.

Tuesday looked miserable. Her face was crumpled, as if she wanted to cry. "Jake, I'm so sorry."

"Come on," said Jake cheerfully. "I've never been hit by a pool ball before. This is a new one for my medical resume."

"It's all my fault. I can't believe that—I wasn't—I wasn't paying attention. I'm a better player than that."

"That's obvious." Jake shook out the ice bag and replaced it on his head. "You're a great player."

No, this was Aidan's fault. He knew that.

Tuesday hadn't been paying attention because Aidan and she had been eye-fucking across a crowded room.

What kind of a brother did that make him, anyway?

A shitty one. "Hey. I can stay on the boat tonight with you." Was it even shittier of him that he wanted to beat Tuesday to the offer?

Probably.

Tuesday lifted her head. "Wait, I can do that."

"You get seasick," said Jake.

She visibly paled. "Crap."

Good. That was good. Aidan stuck his hands in his pockets. "That's settled."

"But do you mind doing me one favor, Aidan?" Jake's voice was a little more strained now, as if pain was setting in.

"Anything."

"Can you drive Tuesday back to the Cat's Claw? We walked from Caprese to the bar. I can pick up my car tomorrow."

"I can walk." Tuesday's words were rushed. "Not a problem. I don't mind. It's not far."

"I'll drive you."

"Night air would clear my head."

Aidan shook his truck keys. "Don't be dumb."

She glared at him, but only reached for Jake's free hand. Once she had it in hers, she didn't seem to know what to do with it. She patted it twice, and then set it back on top of the blanket.

Seemed like Tuesday was as confused as Aidan was.

And he *was* right—there didn't appear to be any connection between her and his brother. That was clear.

Relief was sweet, like cold well water on a parched throat. "If I take you back to the B&B now, I can be back here right when they spring Jake."

She didn't look at him, but she nodded. "Okay."

"Can I have a word with my brother?"

She raised her eyes. "You want to tell him I'm the devil?"

"Something like that." But he softened it with a smile. "I'm right behind you."

Tuesday pressed a quick, careful kiss against Jake's cheek and left through the curtain.

Aidan waited for a few slow ticks of the clock on the wall. An oxygen machine hooked to Jake's finger gave a soft whine until he readjusted his hand.

"Hey. Jake." Aidan bit the inside of his cheek.

"Go for it."

"Huh?" His heart thumped in his chest.

"You guys are ridiculous. It's fine."

"But she chose you."

"She was wrong."

"What if she doesn't agree?"

Jake arched an eyebrow in just the same way Liam did when he couldn't get the business checkbook to balance. "Come on, Aidan. You think we're both imagining it? You're throwing off sparks. So is she."

"Maybe she's just a spark-thrower."

"I held her hand earlier. It felt like holding a small loaf of bread or something. She took it back as soon as possible."

Aidan had held her hand, too, when they'd shook after the game. It had felt like his skin had finally come to life. "Thanks."

"That's kind of a dumb thing to say. It's not like I'm giving her to you. She's a human being. A woman."

Jesus, how he knew that. "I know."

"A woman who happens to be living in your dream house."

"Huh?" A jolt coursed through him.

"Just think about that. Coincidence?"

Later. Aidan would take all of this out later and look at it, think about it, figure out what the hell he was doing. Right now, she waited at his truck for him.

"She and I honestly don't have it." Jake gave a half-smile but kept his eyes closed. "Hurry up and take her home. Don't forget you have to take care of me tonight, though. I expect bagels in the morning, too. And coffee. And your share of the plum muffins. For a week."

CHAPTER FOURTEEN

Tuesday waited next to Aidan's truck. She leaned against the door, trying and failing to take deep breaths of the cold night air. It was chilly enough that she saw her breath when she exhaled. She shivered.

She was overreacting.

That was all.

It had been a very strange night, and now she was taking this too seriously. People probably got brained by pool balls every day all across the nation. Tuesday could remember at least two or three guys who'd been hit by a pool ball, back when she was playing a lot. They usually complained bitterly, especially Matt, who'd been hit in the groin.

But they weren't permanently maimed. She had to let it go, she knew that. Just one more case of her being too concerned with the possibility of hurting someone.

Aidan approached. She took another deep breath of the cold night air and immediately coughed.

"You okay?"

"Choked on my own spit." It was true, but lord, the minute the words were out of her mouth she wanted to reel them back in. *Sexy.*

He gave a half-grin, though. "Hop in."

Aidan opened the truck door for her. It groaned open, and she clambered in without taking the hand he offered.

She needed *not* to touch him.

That wouldn't be so hard, would it?

"He'll be okay, you know." Aidan's hands stayed firmly at two and ten on the wheel.

Tuesday nodded. In her head, she knew it. It didn't stop her heart from worrying, her spirit from deflating.

Aidan took a turn carefully, slowly, as if he were concerned about her being jostled. "I'm more worried about you, honestly."

Startled, Tuesday looked at him. "What?"

His face was lit a low orange from the dashboard, and it should have made him look like a movie monster. Instead, the color just accented the rough stubble on his jaw, the sharp plane of his cheekbone. "No offense, but you're acting like you're the one who got hit."

"I am *not*." Offense, totally taken.

"You're so upset you're practically shaking."

Practically? She folded her hands more tightly in her lap. Her fingers ached with the tension packed into them. "I'm fine."

"Okay. If you say so."

She wasn't fine, course. Apparently that was obvious to him, which was incredibly annoying.

But she wasn't going to tell him why. She didn't owe him that. Did she?

You flirted with him.

She'd been staring at Aidan when she made the shot. Yes, it had been meant to be a jump shot, something she used to be good at. The ball was *not* supposed to jump itself all the way to where Jake stood, though. She hadn't been paying attention—again—and someone had gotten hurt.

She was supposedly an adult. When she'd been a kid, she thought she would have had it together by thirty-three.

It was so far from the truth, it hurt.

The radio was set on low, and Aidan was whistling tunelessly along with an old Dixie Chicks song. He wasn't very good at whistling.

"Sorry," she said.

"Nothing to be sorry for."

So much to be sorry for.

The front window fogged. That was her, she knew it. She could feel herself sweating, and she was breathing shallowly. Aidan cracked his window without comment.

"I appreciate the ride."

"No problem." He glanced at her, and something in the set of his jaw made Tuesday tremble, deep and low inside.

He made her feel reckless. On her side of the truck, they passed a sign that pointed down to the beach.

Danger. Strong current.

Yeah. That was it. "What's the worst thing you've ever done?"

To Aidan's credit, he didn't ask her why she was asking. She didn't know, anyway. "Give me a sec. Let me think about that."

Tuesday uncurled her fingers, shaking them out. Then she sat on her hands and waited.

He signaled his left turn and drove carefully up the street the bed and breakfast was on. He pulled over, switching off his lights. Then he turned off the truck altogether. He stared up toward the street light, which blinked down at them as if unconvinced of the darkness.

Another breath.

Nerves threatened to choke her. Maybe she could choke on her own spit again. That would be amazing. "Never mind. Forget I asked." She reached for the door handle.

"Hang on. It's a good question. I'm still thinking about it. I've done lots of things I regret. Hasn't everyone?"

"Like what?"

"I stole from communion."

"Minor."

"Is it more major if I admit I'm not Catholic?"

Tuesday kept her fingers on the handle. "It's more interesting, anyway."

"And that I picked the lock of the rectory and stole the money right out of Father Josiah's desk? It was tucked in the bank envelope and everything."

"How much?"

"Seventy-two dollars."

"That's all? From Sunday service?"

"The Catholics are all pretty old around here."

"What did you do with the money?"

Looking straight ahead, Aidan smiled. "Bought a pipe for my step-dad Bill. He loved smoking cherry-flavored tobacco."

"No, way. That doesn't count. You robbed from the rich to give to someone you loved. If that's the worst thing you ever did, you should probably apply for sainthood now. Get ready to dry up dead and boring."

"Hey, now. I've done lots of other inappropriate things." He continued to look straight ahead. Thank God. If he looked at her...

"Like?"

Aidan turned it around on her. "What about you? What's the worst thing you've ever done?"

"I'll never tell." She tried to make her voice light but failed.

"Intriguing."

"Nah. Long, boring story." It wasn't—it was short and horrific.

"I broke a girl's heart," he said.

Tuesday frowned. "That's just a thing that happens. We've all broken hearts."

"This one was different."

"I'm sure she recovered."

"She died."

Tuesday let go of the door handle and stared at him. "What?"

"Not from that. It was just really bad timing. I broke up with Willa because she was going away to college. I had to stay here—I could only afford community college then. I didn't want to get in her way of having fun while she was gone." His voice was low and tight. "So I broke up with her even though we were totally in love. I thought it was the high-minded thing to do."

"Plus you wanted to get laid while she was gone," Tuesday guessed.

He shook his head. "I honestly thought we'd get married someday. I thought she was the one. But I was a year older. I thought she should have time to make sure I was the right one for her."

This was more interesting. "Go on."

"I broke up with her, and a day later, she got on the plane to head to New York. From the plane, she left me a voice mail, telling me that she wished we'd never met. That she would rather have never known me than to feel the pain of leaving me."

Did she kill herself? How did a person go on, knowing they might be the cause of that? "What happened to her?"

"The plane crashed. It was that commuter flight, the one from Boston to New York. Sixteen years ago, remember?"

Tuesday did. "That's awful."

"She'd changed her flight to get out of town a day earlier, because she was so broken-hearted."

"That's awful."

"It destroyed me." The words were simple. The emotion in his voice was not—it was a tangled snarl of regret and pain that Tuesday recognized well.

"I'm sorry."

He shrugged and finally looked at her. His eyes were so dark they looked black. "Tell me what you did."

Tuesday opened her mouth, but something the size of a golf ball lodged itself right under her tonsils. She managed, "Sorry. I'm exhausted." She pushed the door open and hurled herself out of the car. She tripped on the sidewalk. She felt drunk even though she knew she hadn't had enough alcohol to affect her this way.

Aidan was out of the truck and around to her side before she could even reach the three low steps that led to the Cat's Claw porch. "Wait. I scared you."

Him? He hadn't scared her. She was too busy scaring herself. "It's fine. I'm sorry that happened to you. I'm sorry I asked—"

Aidan caught her hands in his. He was suddenly so close that she felt the air get thin in her lungs, as if he'd hauled her to a mountaintop without her looking. "I'm glad you did."

"Aidan—" She couldn't do this. She couldn't flirt with him anymore. It wasn't fair to anyone.

"Pick me."

She blinked. No appropriate words formed in her brain—she only found a vast blankness where words used to live.

"Tuesday, pick me instead. You don't feel this with Jake. I know you don't."

Of course she didn't.

Jake was vanilla. Jake was a space heater.

Aidan was chili powder. He was a volcano.

"I can't. I made my choice. It wouldn't be—" It wouldn't be right? It wouldn't be fair? What in life was?

"Just—let me—"

"What? Just let you what?" She should pull back her hands, but she didn't want to—not quite yet. Another second, and she'd be able to go inside. Another half second. Okay, one more.

He didn't ask—he just moved.

Aidan's mouth dropped to hers. Tuesday should have seen it coming, should have read it in his eyes, but she hadn't, and the feeling of his lips was a surprise. She would have gasped but she lacked the breath, and she might not ever get it back. He'd bent his knees as he moved in to her, swooping an arm around her back, and she sagged against it, grateful that he'd caught her, because in her surprise, she might have sunk all the way to the step.

To make up for being off-balance, she swung an arm around his neck. She could have pushed against his chest to catch herself. She could have pressed him away.

But she didn't.

Instead, Tuesday kissed him back.

That was where the real trouble began.

He was heat incarnate. Just the feeling of his lips on hers made her tremble, a fine jitter setting up shop inside her bones. His tongue slipped inside her mouth to touch hers, and nothing had ever tasted this way in the history of humanity. He tasted of desire, of fire, of lust, and of something rich and deep and sweet, like chocolate melted over a low flame.

Tuesday wanted more.

She pressed herself against him, her breasts pushing against his hard chest. He took a half step forward, pressing his knee between her legs, and she met him, moving her hips forward. Aidan growled low in his throat and the vibration in her mouth made her suddenly slippery with need. She could kiss him all night—no, for the rest of her life—

The porch light clicked on overhead with a snap.

Tuesday shoved herself away from him, blinking like a mole caught by the sun. In the window to the left of the door, the curtain shook, and she caught the fleeting image of Pearl Hawthorne frowning out at them.

"Busted." Aidan smiled. His lips shined with wetness.

"Damn it." Tuesday didn't know what was a bigger disappointment—the fact that they'd been caught or the fact that she'd kissed him back. "I—"

"Look. Just pick me instead of Jake. We—" he pointed at her and then back at himself "—we have this, this whatever it is."

"It's too late." She wouldn't do that to Jake. That would just be a crappy thing to do, to anyone.

"Jake said it's okay."

Tuesday stared. "Pardon?" It was the voice she used in the classroom when a student had just insulted someone else's religion. Even fifth graders, as cocky as they often were, couldn't stand up to Tuesday's *Pardon*.

But Aidan could, apparently. "Yeah. We talked about it."

"You talked about me. About *me*?"

The corner of his mouth quirked. She wanted to touch it, that place where it dipped. She balled her hands into fists. "When?"

"After you went out to the truck to wait for me."

"You were like thirty seconds behind me." Tuesday folded her arms across her chest. "It was that easy."

He shrugged, that entirely inappropriate grin still threatening to show itself. "Sure."

"He didn't mind at all."

"Are your feelings hurt?"

Hell, yes, they were hurt. She shouldn't have been kissing Aidan—it was the wrong thing to do—and Jake totally should have still wanted to date her. "Not at all."

"They are. Do you still want to date him for the show?"

She should say yes. Just to show Aidan that she wasn't a tool in his toolbox that could be swapped out or exchanged at will.

But holy crap, she wanted to kiss the man in front of her some more. A lot. "I'll think about it."

"You do that." A light danced in his eyes.

Cheeky, that's what her mother would call this man. Completely cheeky. "I might not switch."

"Totally your call. We're working for the network."

"And for me."

He dipped his head and touched his forehead. "At your service." He raised his eyes and met hers. "And I mean that. I am completely, totally at your service."

"Oh, my God." It was a breath. Tuesday reached out to touch the wall, just to prove she was still in charge of her own body.

"I'll see you tomorrow," Aidan said.

At the house. Yes, at the house. "Wait, on a Saturday?"

"Round the clock is how the network likes it. And they pay overtime."

Tuesday nodded briefly.

The porch light flickered off and then on again.

"I'm going inside."

"You do that."

"You don't have to tell me what to do."

He grinned wider, and lord, she wanted to reach forward and dig her fingers into his shirt, drawing his mouth to hers again.

No.

Pull it together.

She nodded once, and pushed the door. Thankfully, it opened at her touch, and she didn't have to find the keys.

She'd wanted it light. She'd wanted to date Jake because he was safe. Easy. She wouldn't have had to worry about him.

Aidan was an explosion ready to happen.

Tuesday wasn't sure she had the bravery to light the match.

CHAPTER FIFTEEN

Aidan got to the site bright and early.

So bright. And so early.

It was barely five after six when he pulled up to the old Callahan house, and he'd already been awake for two hours. After that little sleep, he should be in a bear of a mood, but he wasn't. If he were the kind of guy who skipped, he would have done it, all the way up the long driveway. But he wasn't, so he satisfied himself with whistling loudly as he went up the porch steps, lugging the box of donuts as he went. He slapped the side of door as he entered. *Hello, you beautiful thing.*

For one second, he allowed himself to imagine Tuesday. Living in this house.

With him.

It was such an idiotic idea—he knew that firmly, deeply. He knew it all the way to his bones.

But he also knew that the thought was something that made him feel almost...hopeful.

Tuesday wouldn't be here yet, he told himself. She'd sleep in, probably. Maybe she'd dream a little of him. Yeah,

Aidan liked the image that brought to his mind. Her in bed—did she sleep naked?—rolling over, waking to the memory of kissing him. Maybe she'd touch her lips, maybe she'd touch herself lower...

Nope, nope, *nope. Think about something else.* He thought about the way his favorite saw had rusted when he'd accidentally left it outside five years back. Instant bone-killer. He needed to keep it PG if he was going to do any honest work today.

"Hey! I got donuts!"

He heard a few grumbles from the kitchen where his crew had been tearing out a wall (the correct one). They were just settling in, dropping jackets in the corner, plugging in power saws and unrolling plans. "Here you go."

"Thanks." Socal, who stayed thin and angular no matter what she ate, reached for a glazed cream-filled.

Sturgeon lunged forward and grabbed a jelly donut, but Bass hung back. The fish boys were best friends, with no higher ambition that getting through the work day safely so they could go smoke a joint while fishing on their days off. They were sweet and not-so-smart but both were incredibly handy, and they didn't mind doing the heavy grunt work. Their nicknames had been given to them as kids, and were so stuck to them now that Aidan couldn't ever remember what their legal names were. Liam knew—he cut the checks—but Aidan didn't care.

"What's up, Bass?" Aidan waved a hand. "The maple glazed I just ate was still a little warm."

Socal gave a happy moan. "Mine is, too."

Bass shook his head. "I'm gluten-free."

Sturgeon pushed his ball cap back and stared. "Since when."

"Like, a long time."

"How long?"

"Like, two weeks."

Sturgeon scowled. "Since you started dating that Cindy girl."

"That's not it."

"She's what, a vegan?"

"Don't say that."

"It's true! What are you gonna do next, give up fishing?"

Bass stared at Sturgeon as if he'd stabbed him. "I can't believe you just *said* that to me."

"If the shoe fits..."

Socal shook her donut in the air, catching the spilling cream with one finger. "Children. Let mommy eat her donut."

Aidan snorted. "Mommy needs to tell me how the kitchen's going."

Socal gave a visible shudder. "I already regret saying that word out loud. Okay, we've got the old cabinets out and the fish boys took them over to Zach's workshop. He doesn't think there's much worth saving, but he'll give it his best shot. We haven't found the right countertops yet."

"No marble?"

"Tuesday told Felicia she was kidding about that."

Huh.

Socal shrugged. "Felicia said she'd be back in a little while to get you on camera talking about the top floor, but she disappeared, and I'm honestly not sure where she is. I gotta say, she looked a little green."

"Green?"

"Like she has the flu or something. If she does, can you tell her to stay out of the kitchen? I'm planning on eating nothing but donuts today, and that'll lower my immune system."

"Eat some regular food, then."

"Hell, no." Socal stuck out her arms. "Put the whole box in Mommy's arm so she can cradle it." She shivered. "That's the creepiest thing I've ever said. And I can't believe I haven't been saying it this whole time. The look on your face is *priceless*."

Aidan pushed the box her direction and went to look for Felicia. Luckily, the network never had any interest in the *actual* construction part. They wanted a few shots of the buyer and whoever she was dating doing some work. In one episode, the buyer had painted the front door (badly—they'd had to redo it when the cameras left). In another, the buyer had "helped" replaster the laundry room ceiling, and had gotten a glob of topcoat in her eye. The show had made that uneventful visit to the ER into an "I almost died" segment. Really, she'd just needed her eyeball rinsed out.

"Felicia?" She wasn't on the first floor, and she didn't appear to be in the backyard. He headed upstairs.

"Anyone up here?" he called.

"Go away." A small voice came from the end of the hallway.

She didn't sound right. Aidan hurried to the bathroom door. "Felicia?"

"I'm fine."

He knocked. "Come on, let me in."

A groan was his answer.

The door was unlocked.

Felicia sat on the floor. Her face, normally perfectly made-up, was pale and sweaty. Her shirt was unbuttoned, showing her tank top underneath. She rested with her forehead on the rim of the seat.

"That looks truly unhygienic, and I eat at the hot dog place on the way to Eureka."

"Oh, God," she groaned, raising her head.

"Where's Liam?"

"At the office."

Aidan pulled out his cell. "I'm calling him."

"No!" She held up a hand. "I'm fine."

"You're so not fine. You need to go to the doctor. Or home to bed, at a minimum."

"Aidan." Her voice sounded desperate. "I'm really fine. I promise you."

"What—this is just morning sickness or something?"

Her face gave her away.

"Holy shit. You're pregnant." Something dropped away in his stomach.

She dropped her head again. "We were going to tell you and Jake together. Oh, God, Liam will be so disappointed I told you."

"Oh, my God. Congratulations." He should have seen this coming. Why hadn't he? Liam was the oldest. He was *supposed* to fall in love, get married, and have a baby before Aidan and Jake did.

That was life.

That was the *good* life.

Jealousy? Of his brother's perfect set up?

That was some bullshit, and he was a better man than that.

"I think the worst is over."

He held out his hand. "Can you stand up?"

Felicia nodded. He helped her up, her palm clammy and cold in his. He ran the water in the sink till it was hot, and then handed her two paper towels from the roll that had been tossed in the tub.

Then, after she'd washed and dried her face and hands, when he was sure she wasn't going to drop into another crouch, he hugged her.

"Congratulations, sister." He'd never called her that before. "I'm so happy for you two."

Felicia gave a soft hiccup and pulled away. "Thank you."

"You're excited." It wasn't a question.

"I'm terrified. But yeah, we're excited. Liam can't stand it—we were going to tell you both tonight, I swear it. We've only known for a day or two. It's still early, we're not telling anyone else yet."

A creak of the floorboards made them look toward the doorway, but there was no one there.

CHAPTER SIXTEEN

Tuesday backed quietly down the hall, tiptoeing until she reached the far end, then she went as quietly down the stairs as she could. She made her way into the living room, where drop cloths protected the hardwood from the sawdust that drifted everywhere. She pressed her hands to her face.

She shouldn't have eavesdropped. She hadn't *meant* to. She'd been looking for Aidan—why? To thank him for the donuts? It was a thin excuse, but one she'd been planning on using anyway—and when she'd heard Aidan say *Holy shit*, she'd gotten closer, concerned.

Felicia Turbinado, the showrunner, was pregnant.

She was Liam Ballard's girlfriend. It sounded like they were happy about the pregnancy.

Great.

Tuesday closed her eyes.

It really was great. For Felicia and Liam and their whole family, it was going to be an amazing thing.

Tuesday just had to face facts—that unless she moved to a nunnery, she'd be around pregnant women at some point. She thought about the satisfied, almost greedy way women kept a hand on their belly when they were pregnant. As if they needed to telegraph their status, as if they worried people might just think they were fat. Did they ever stop to think of the pain they were causing, just by their very existence?

Of course they didn't.

Tuesday was the freak show, the problem, the broken one.

Not them.

Diana, they're everywhere.

Diana had two little ones of her own. Right at this moment, all the way across the country, she was probably busy doing something for them. That's what she was best at.

Tuesday would never send the email to her ex-best friend.

Anyway, the work on this show would take less than a month, so they were almost halfway through already. Felicia wouldn't even be showing by the time it was done. Hopefully it would continue to be a secret, and Tuesday could pretend she knew nothing.

It was a small town, though, and Felicia had already been sweet to her. Tuesday had liked her, too. She'd been happy that this network executive, the one she'd be working most closely with, was actually a resident in town.

She was the partner of one of the Ballard Brothers. They'd met and fallen in love on TV.

Tuesday had come to Darling Bay for a new life, for the house of her dreams. *For escape.* The dating she'd have to do on the show was something she hadn't worried about—she'd just go on the dates, and then her house would be done to her exact specifications, and then she'd live in this new-to-her sweet, small town.

As she decided on the next step in her life, she'd hang out with new friends.

Like Felicia. That's what she had hoped, anyway.

"Hey, you." Aidan's voice came from behind her. "When did you get here?"

She stuck a plastic smile on her lips—the one she'd used in the classroom when parents yelled at her, disappointed that she hadn't given Johnny an A for not doing a lick of work all year. "Just a second ago."

He wore a denim jacket with a black corduroy collar. His tool belt hung from his hips, and his wide hands hung at his sides. His eyes were smoky, and there were dark circles under his eyes.

Had he not slept much, either? Tuesday had kept falling into sleep, but her dreams were full of his hands, his lips, the sound of his voice.

"Hey," he said again. He smiled, and the warmth reached those dark blue eyes of his. How did he not have a squad of women flocking at his heels, hoping for just one of those grins?

To be fair, Felicia *was* behind him. "Hi, Tuesday. Aidan said there're donuts in the kitchen." A wave of chartreuse swept up her cheeks. Weakly, she added, "You should go have one."

"Are you okay?" It would have looked suspicious not to ask.

Felicia touched her stomach. "A touch of food poisoning, I think. We had clams last night. Maybe that's it. I bet that's what it is. I think."

She was a bad liar. Not like Tuesday, who lied boldfaced to one of the producers when still in the selection process nodded. *Yes, I'm absolutely okay with the idea of falling in love on camera. Yes, I'm open to marriage. Yes, I'm open to having children.* "Of course. You should go home and rest."

Felicia tugged the bottom of her tank top. "A little more coffee, and I'll be right as rain. We're going to do some new walk-through takes with Aidan and you in about thirty minutes, that okay? Since this lug saw fit to hammer his way through the wall that needed to stay in the kitchen, we can't really use that footage."

Aidan grimaced. "I thought I was helping."

"You did not. You were mad." Felicia flicked a look at her watch. "I've got to find Anna. Meet me back here at eight?"

Tuesday nodded. So did Aidan.

Felicia left the room, taking all the air with her.

Tuesday felt the top of her lungs contract. She wouldn't look right at him. No.

But it was like when she was little, when her mother had told her not to look directly at the partial eclipse. After she'd heard the order, she'd wanted nothing so much as to look. So Tuesday had. She hadn't been able to see anything around the bright burn on her retina for an hour afterward.

Aidan felt that bright. Then he smiled at her again, and the wattage went up by a million. "So, have you thought more about dumping Jake?"

CHAPTER SEVENTEEN

Tuesday had thought about it. With little resolution. She *wanted* to choose Aidan—she wanted badly to pick him. "I've thought about it," she started.

"Yeah?"

"I want to know something. Why were you so mad that day you beat the wall with a mallet?"

"It was a sledgehammer, and I wasn't angry with you."

"Yes, you were. I could tell."

He shook his head slowly, and his eyes bored into hers. "I swear to you. I wasn't mad at you. I was angry at a situation."

"What situation?"

"One that's changed a little now."

"How?"

"I kissed you."

Her scar felt hot under her shirt. "No, that's not it. You wanted to run me out of town, and then you change your mind, just like that? It makes me nervous."

"That I want to see more of you than just on the job site? Makes me nervous, too."

Yeah, right. Everything about the confident Aidan—from the top of his dark brown hair to the tips of dusty work boots—made her feel skittish. Once, when she was young, she'd adopted a feral kitten who would only come to her in her sleep, when she was as still as possible. Tuesday would wake up, the cat curled warmly into her side, but the second she moved, the cat was gone.

Tuesday felt like the cat, her nerves on red alert. She longed to say *yes*. But if he moved too quickly, said a word that was halfway wrong, she'd skitter sideways out of the room. Maybe out of the state.

Jake had been safe.

Aidan was not.

"I'll let you know later today."

She expected him to protest. To push. Instead, he ducked his head. "Sounds good." He looked out the window behind her. "You have a fairy in your garden, did you know that?"

"Oh!" The long-haired girl she'd seen the first day at the garden gate was back. This time she was all the way in the yard. Her dress was green this time, and her tights were blue. Same orange sneakers. The girl stood with her arms crossed, staring up at the house as if waiting for someone. "I want to talk to her. You said her name's Ella?"

He nodded.

"Will you call me when it's time to do the filming?"

"Yeah. Sure."

Tuesday made her way down through the busy kitchen and onto the back porch.

The girl started. She turned to run back to the gate that was still ajar.

"Wait!"

The girl froze, one leg in her own yard, the rest of her body in Tuesday's.

"I'm your new neighbor." Tuesday hurried down the grassy slope, past the weed-choked raised beds. "You're Ella, right?"

The girl turned slowly. "I didn't mean to trespass."

"You're not."

"Are you sure?" The girl rubbed at her neck. A long red scar, crinkled and thick, ran from her jaw into the top of her green smock.

Tuesday forced her eyes away from the puckered skin. She nodded. "You're only trespassing if you're not allowed somewhere. And you're allowed."

"I am?"

"Sure. We're neighbors. I'm Tuesday Willis." She saw a thin blue vein jump in the girl's throat right next to the scar.

"Tuesday?"

"I know, it's weird, right?"

The girl nodded, her brown eyes wide in her thin face. "Why did you get it?"

"My name?"

Another nod.

"My dad's a very literal guy. I was born on a Tuesday. You know the rhyme? Tuesday's child is full of grace?"

Ella looked at her blankly.

"And he thought it would be sort of funny."

"It is funny."

Tuesday sighed. "Tell me about it."

"Did kids make fun of you? I met a boy called Grape once and he said everyone made fun of him all the time."

"Yep. I got teased a lot."

The girl blinked solemnly.

Tuesday took a careful step forward. Clunky orange shoes aside, the child seemed ethereal, as if she might melt into mist any second. "And you're Ella. Like Cinder?"

Ella rolled her eyes, and Tuesday was relieved to see she really was a human child, not a garden figment. "Everyone says that."

"Do you hate it?"

"*Yes.* Cinderella's not even a good character."

"Why?"

"She just runs away? Why? If she wanted the prince to love her, she just had to be herself anyway. She could have changed back into herself at midnight that first night, and the whole kingdom search never would have happened."

Probably because the prince wouldn't have been interested once he got to know the real girl. "You live next door?"

A nod.

"Can I peek?" Tuesday gestured to the gate.

Another nod.

Through the gate and up a low rise stood a small green cottage. It had old gray shutters that might have been white once, and a tiny Miata sports car sat rusting next to a clothesline. The top was down, and looked like it had been for years. A slight smell of burnt matches, or overcooked eggs, hung in the air. "It looks..." Tuesday wasn't sure what to say.

"It looks like no one lives there."

"You're right." The way the brown grass was overgrown, the way the screen door hung, only halfway attached.

"Mom says she keeps it that way on purpose. But I'm not sure that's the real reason."

"Why would she want that?"

"She says so people don't come to the house and bother me while she's at work."

"She's at work a lot?"

Ella's lips closed, as if she'd suddenly remembered she wasn't supposed to talk to strangers.

"Forget I asked. That was a rude question."

The girl appeared surprised, her dark eyebrows lifting. "My mom says I'm full of rude questions."

"Oh, good, they're my favorite."

Ella giggled. "How old are you?"

"How old do you think I am?"

Tilting her head, Ella considered. "Fifty."

"Wow! No."

"Twenty-one?"

"Flatterer. I'm thirty-three. How old are you?"

"How old do *you* think I am?"

Tuesday considered. She was tall enough to be twelve, but she had a young demeanor. "I think you're eleven."

Ella blinked. "How did you know?"

"I'm a teacher."

"What grade?"

"Fifth. Usually." Who knew what she'd teach in the future? If anything? "Are you in sixth?"

Ella nodded. "I hate it."

"Why?"

"Because we're doing geometry and my teacher doesn't even care that I don't understand it."

"What don't you understand?"

"Any of it. I sometimes get the answers right because I can kind of guess angles with my stupid protractor. But I can never remember how to tell if something's acute or obtuse. I don't know why, and that's driving me *crazy*."

Tuesday didn't laugh, even though the little girl most definitely sounded like an adult on the last few words. Undoubtedly, her mother said something similar, often. "The word acute has the word cut in it. A sharp angle can cut you, so an angle that looks like a blade is acute."

"Oh!" Ella looked surprised.

"Your teacher never taught you that?"

"No, no." Ella waved her hands. "Can you help me?"

Tuesday took a step backward. "Um."

"Please? You're our neighbor, so you're not a stranger. Mom won't mind. I like being around you."

The words were simple and sweet, going straight to Tuesday's blood like sparkling wine. "You do?"

Ella shrugged. "Sometimes it happens fast."

Tuesday thought of Aidan. "Sometimes it does."

"So you'll help me? With geometry?"

"Ella, I—" Tuesday should say no. She wasn't ready. But she didn't know how to say it without bursting this girl's hopeful bubble.

The girl was intuitive, that much was clear. She stopped. Immediately. As if Tuesday had yelled at her instead of just stammering.

"Never mind," Ella said.

"Wait—"

But Ella was already retreating, her hand covering her neck. "S'fine."

"Ella." Tuesday reached a hand forward. "It's not—"

"Not about my scar," Ella muttered. "I know." She reached for the latch of the gate.

"Your *scar?*" Oh, no. Tuesday wasn't going to let that one go. She hurried, taking long steps, and managed to get next to the girl. "You think this is about your scar?"

Ella rolled her eyes. "It was from a pan of spaghetti water, I was three, I pulled it down on myself, and I don't remember it at all. No, it will never go away. No, it doesn't still hurt."

Tuesday pulled up her shirt, exposing her stomach.

Ella gasped.

Tuesday took a breath and felt the cool air hit all the parts of her skin that weren't knotted and roped by the thickened skin. "I don't care about your scar."

Ella covered her mouth with her fingers.

"Yeah?" Tuesday wanted to drop the hem of her shirt, but Ella's eyes were huge, taking it all in.

"That's a bad one."

"It's still pretty fresh, that's why it's still so angry looking."

"How long?"

"About eight months." It was hard to believe. The crash felt like yesterday and at the same time, it was forever ago.

"Does it still itch?"

"All the time. Does yours?"

Ella looked surprised to be asked. "No. But I kind of remember that it did. Sometimes I still scratch it."

"They told me not to."

"Yeah, well." Ella sighed and she sounded twenty years older. She pointed at Tuesday's torso. "Are you okay? Like, inside?"

Strangely, she couldn't lie to this kid. "I can't have children. Other than that, I'm okay." So very not okay.

"Do you mind?"

"Yes."

"That sucks."

It was nice to hear, actually. "Agreed." Tuesday let the hem of her shirt drop. "I just wanted you to know you're not alone."

"Thanks." The girl's gaze fell to the ground.

"What is it?"

"Well, it's just that yours...no one can see yours."

That was true. In most cases, Tuesday's scar was invisible to the world. Ella's scar, unless she wore a turtleneck—did they even make those anymore?—was on view to the world. "That must be really hard on you."

Ella's eyes widened. "It *is*."

"Why do you look so surprised that I say that?"

"Because grownups always say it's not a big deal. That I should just ignore it. Mom says I should not care that I have it, that it makes me strong."

Tuesday could feel her mother's gaze on her own face as she lay in the hospital bed. *Don't worry, darling, no one will see that. And if they do, no one will care. You lived through it. You're stronger now.*

"Well, they're not the ones with the scar, huh?"

Ella grinned. "They're *not*."

"We are, though."

"We *are*." She held out her closed fist.

Tuesday stared at it for a moment.

Oh.

She fist-bumped the girl gently.

"Scar club!" said Ella.

"Scar club."

"Bye!"

In two steps, she was through the gate, and when Tuesday moved to call her back, she wasn't even in her yard—she'd disappeared into the house with a quiet bang.

Damn it. She wasn't ready for a friendship with a kid. Not yet.

Unless that kid was Ella... Maybe?

Ella was right about one thing, though. Sometimes things did happen fast.

CHAPTER EIGHTEEN

Felicia rounded up Aidan just as he was coming up from under the house. Tuesday was with her, and Aidan spent a good five seconds thumping his ball cap against his leg to get the dust from under the house off it.

Felicia flipped a page of her notebook. "How does it look down there?"

He pressed his hands to his lower back and straightened as much as he could. "It's good. Foundation is fixed, and we earthquake retrofitted it, too. Now we're ready to do the rest of the work inside."

Felicia snapped her fingers toward Gene. "Sorry, Aidan, can you say that again? On camera?"

He did, feeling like an idiot. Why did they even call it reality TV? There was nothing real about it.

Except for the way his heart beat sped up whenever Tuesday entered a room. That was, well—that was *really* fucking real.

"That's good," said Tuesday. "That'll save us money, right?"

She was great on camera. A natural. "You'd think so, yeah, but unfortunately I found that the floor of the bathroom is pretty rotted through. There was a leak in the bathtub overflow valve, and water's been pooling underneath the tub for years."

Tuesday pushed her hair back out of her face. "That explains the moldy smell. I was hoping that was just stagnant water in the pipes."

"Nope."

Her face fell. His fault. "I can fix it, though."

"For a lot more money. I know."

"Nah. It'll still come in under the estimate." Liam was going to kill him.

But the way her face had brightened made his forthcoming death worth it.

Felicia gave him a skeptical look, her right eyebrow arched. She gestured at the camera again. "Can you please tell Tuesday why you think you'll be able to save her money?"

Felicia was just being nice. She was trying to push the Ballard Brother brand—they liked to under-promise and over-deliver, coming in under budget when they could.

"If it was my house—" he started. It wasn't. That was the whole problem. God, it was complicated. How did he give advice to a woman who owned the house of his dreams?

"Yeah?" Tuesday leaned forward. He could smell her perfume, light and clean, like sunshine on wild mustard blossoms.

"If I was redoing the place for myself—" he cleared his throat "—I'd tear out this downstairs bathroom, and make it bigger. Make a place for a clawfoot, since the floor can handle the weight. Tankless water heater. Redo the whole subfloor, maybe even bring in geothermal."

"Geothermal what—water?"

"Heat, yeah. You could pipe the whole house with it, but that would be pretty expensive. But just to bring it in here on one level, to heat the floors in winter, that would be easy."

Tuesday shook her head. Her cheeks were so pink and her lips so full—he wanted to taste them again, the cameras be damned. "I still don't get it. Geothermal from where?"

He stared. "You know about the hot springs."

"What?"

Felicia laughed. "Whoops."

Aidan stared at Tuesday. "That is *literally* the best thing about this house." And it would have been a perfect house even without the spring. "There's a natural hot pool at the bottom of the yard. Part of a chain of them on this side of town. And you didn't know?"

"That's the rotten egg smell in the backyard?"

"Yeah."

"But where is it?"

"In the shared easement below your fence. You saw the gate, right?"

"Only the one that leads next door."

"Oh, my God, let's go." He saw Felicia shoot a thumb's up at Gene and his camera, but he ignored the TV crew as they followed on their heels. The fact that he got to show Tuesday the best part of the property made him feel giddy, like he was in his hang glider, soaring down toward the water and then banking back up again.

She was going to love this.

CHAPTER NINETEEN

T uesday *had* seen something about a spring in the contract, and she'd meant to ask, but in her mind it was like the old wells in the backyards of older Duluth properties. They were capped. Dangerous. Ignored.

She never imagined a geothermal hot spring. Of her *own*.

The gate was hidden by the overgrown vines. No wonder Tuesday hadn't seen it before. As it was, Aidan had to hack their way through a couple of thick branches of it in order to creak it open. She was impressed that he had a folding saw on his person. He dug it out of his tool belt, put on goggles, and sawed away.

"This is wisteria, right?"

Aidan nodded. He pulled on the gate. One more vine in the way. It almost hurt to watch him work. Firstly, the way his triceps flexed as he sawed was probably illegal in some parts of the country. He looked like a Greek God. He should have been on the side of an urn somewhere.

Secondly, it was *wisteria*. "Won't that hurt the plant?"

"Yeah. It will."

"Do we have to?" She winced as he finished breaking off a large overhang of thick vine.

"Oh, darlin'. You're going to be so happy I did."

His voice was pitched low, just for her (though of course Anna had her boom mic up—it hung over their heads like a fat squirrel on a pole). His words made Tuesday shiver.

She waited as he finished sawing. The gate to the neighbor's yard squeaked once, as if Ella might be checking on them, but it didn't open, and Tuesday didn't look. She'd scared the girl once—she didn't need to again.

"Is there just one? Hot spring?"

Aidan flipped the narrow saw closed and took out a pocketknife. "There are lots of them, all along this ridge. Most of them are private, like this one, but some are on public land. I can't believe you've never heard of them."

"I'm from Minnesota."

He sawed cheerfully at several more vines that had wound around the gate's handle. "So?"

"Apparently I know nothing about the whole state. I thought California was all white sand and bright sun and palm trees." She hadn't known it could get dark and rainy. She hadn't known it would be so thickly forested.

She hadn't known the man she couldn't take her eyes off would look like one of the men who hunted in the Superior national forest.

"You disappointed?" Aidan put the pocketknife between his teeth and untangled the last vine, which appeared to have tied itself in a knot.

She didn't answer. She wasn't. She just didn't know how to say it.

Aidan slipped the knife back into his pocket and pulled open the gate.

He waved his arm. "If you are, this should fix it."

Tuesday's favorite book as a child had been The Secret Garden. When Mary Lennox's robin led her in, when the door had opened, nine-year-old Tuesday had gasped. She hadn't been in her bed with snow falling outside, so much of it that school had closed, but she'd been in England with Colin and Dickon, making the garden beautiful. As an adult, she read it to her class just before every winter break. Her copy was dog-eared, the cover limp. She loved that book and its fictional garden fiercely.

The hot spring was even better than that.

The gate opened to a rugged staircase that led down into a little clearing. A natural grotto made of rock outcroppings stood in a semi-circle. Tall trees grew in a ring, twenty feet away from the water—redwoods and a couple of pine. But right around the pool were just low, flat rocks covered with a mossy carpet.

The water glittered, dark and sparkling.

It was triple the size of the biggest hot tub at her parents' YMCA. But there were no safety warnings, no lifeguards. No concrete, no wall clocks. Just the rocks, and the high blue sky above. A white plume of steam rose— wider at the middle of the pool, dissipating at the edges. The wind soughed in the branches and a chirruping came from a fat squirrel perched halfway up a sycamore. The air smelled strongly of pine leaves, and mildly of rotten eggs.

She loved it.

"What do you think?" She felt Aidan's careful eyes on her.

"Oh." It was all Tuesday could say. She knew the cameras were on her—she *knew* they'd probably use this footage—and she didn't care. Happy tears came to her eyes, hot and surprising. This was hers, this was home, this was incredible. "Oh."

Behind them, Felicia laughed. "How are you feeling about the property now?"

"This is seriously part of the property? You're sure."

Aidan's lips tightened for a split second, but the smile stayed in his eyes. "Yep."

"Is it safe? Or is it one of those boiling pools that'll take your skin off?" She'd read about the ones in Iceland—pools in which a person could actually boil eggs for dinner.

"It's about a hundred degrees on the edge and a couple degrees hotter in the middle."

"Oh," she said again.

It was magical.

A tiny forest grove with a hot pool of her very own. She would move down here, abandon the house and set up housekeeping here. All she would need was a hammock and a box full of trail mix. She'd read books by the side of the spring, and she'd slip in when she got cold. She would forget to worry about all that had happened in the past, and all that might happen in the future. This was a perfect place to be alone.

Or with one other person.

She looked at Aidan. Her heart skittered in her chest, as if she'd tried to skip it across the flat water. "Have you been in this pool before?"

He'd been looking over the water, but his gaze slammed into hers a split second after she'd spoken. "Yeah. A teacher of mine lived here, and sometimes we'd go in after dinner."

"Nice."

Aidan looked at the cameras. He looked at Felicia. "Let's take a dip."

Surprise rippled down her arms. "What?"

"Let's get in." His hands went to his tool belt. Unceremoniously, he dropped it to the moss.

"Now?"

"No better time."

"I don't have a swimsuit." It was a weak protest.

"You got on underwear?"

Oh, yes. She did. She'd never admit she'd purposefully chosen her newest black bra and panty set that morning. She hadn't been thinking that he would see it, but she'd chosen it nonetheless, ignoring the fact that she'd thought of Aidan while she'd done up the bra clasp. "Of course I do."

"Same thing as a suit. Come on."

Felicia looked surprised. "Aidan, are you sure?"

Tuesday realized she'd made up her mind last night. It just hadn't sunk in till this moment. "Felicia?" She tried to keep her hands from shaking.

Felicia was looking at her pad of paper, flipping the pages as if she could find the script they were obviously deviating from. "Yeah?"

"I've decided I'm going to date Aidan. Not Jake."

Felicia dropped her notebook. The pages slapped the air at her feet. "Sorry?"

Aidan gave a brief whoop and then whipped off his shirt. His chest looked better than it had in Tuesday's imagination, which was saying a *lot*. His abs were taut, defined. A fine trail of dark hair led to the top of his jeans, where his fingers worked on his belt. Both shoulders were covered in thick blue ink, something she hadn't expected. Tribal bands, and something else—a bird of prey of some sort crept over his shoulders.

Tuesday wanted to get closer. She wanted to turn him around, to inspect him, inch by inch. Her heart beat in her throat. "It's okay. Jake and Aidan talked about it. Jake doesn't mind." It didn't feel *good*, exactly, that Jake was so willing to give her up, but it was perfect that Aidan wanted to be the one she dated instead.

"Are you *sure* about that?" Felicia picked up her pad of paper and made a hand motion at the nearest camera.

Aidan's shirt was at his feet, and his jeans were going next. "What she's saying is that Liam's the brain and Jake's the looks. I'm just the meathead who hits things with hammers."

"I'm sure." With every step he took to being clothesless, Tuesday was getting more sure. She wanted to date him on camera, whatever that entailed.

And what about off-camera? Silver bits of lightning swam in her stomach, like tiny fish that wanted to get back to the water.

She peeled down her jeans, speeding up to match Aidan's pace. He already stood in dark blue boxers decorated with...was that the Captain America logo? "Come on, gorgeous," he said, sitting on the rock, putting his legs in the water.

The boxers surprised her more than his endearment. Combined, they nearly stopped her heart completely. He waded farther in, walking backward, watching her.

Tuesday shucked her shoes and finished taking off her jeans. She was down to her panties, but decided against taking off her T-shirt. Her butt in underwear was one thing. Her scar on display for the world to see was another.

Panties are just like bikini bottoms. Panties are just like bikini bottoms. She could *feel* everyone staring.

She could feel *Aidan* staring. Oh, God.

So she closed her eyes and sat on the rock. She swung in her legs and concentrated on the feeling of the hot water lapping up her thighs. The bottom, soft with silty sand, dropped away quickly, and she bent her knees, going up to her neck.

It was fresh-bathtub hot. When she extended her toes forward, toward the center where Aidan already floated, she could feel the extra degrees of heat in front of her.

Tension she hadn't known she was holding loosened, leaving her shoulders. Her neck popped as she stretched it to one side, then the other. She dog-paddled lazily and turned around to find—of course—that every pair of eyeballs and camera lenses were aimed at her.

Every pair of eyes but Aidan's. His back was now to her as he waded farther in, ten feet in front of her. Her foot grazed a submerged rock, and she stood on it, out of the water to her waist. "Aidan." She didn't have a follow-up sentence planned. She just wanted to say his name.

He turned to face her.

His eyes were naked with hunger.

Tuesday gasped and slipped on the rock, plunging back into the hot water.

Was that look for her?

She ducked under, the heat prickling her scalp. She held her nose and stayed under the water for a long five-count, then she spluttered back up. She'd forgotten about her glasses, as usual, and she took them off and shook them hard before replacing them.

He was probably literally hungry.

That was it.

He liked her. Yes. That had been established. That's all it was.

She turned to face him again, and it took everything she had to smile. Casual. She could be relaxed, right? She was in a hot tub in California! Wasn't this what people did?

The craving had left his face. He just looked like Aidan again. She felt equal parts relief and disappointment.

He smiled at her and moved her direction. When he was three feet away from her, he called over her head, "Hey, Felicia!"

"Yeah?" Felicia was saying something to Anna and Gene, her voice intense.

"You okay with the brother swap?"

"Sure. What do I care? I have the brother I want."

"Good." Aidan's voice was strong as a tree trunk, rough as its bark. "At least you'll get our second kiss on camera."

Tuesday's heart hammered in her ears, and she wasn't sure if it was the heat that was making her entire body one long flush or him.

No, she knew.

It was definitely him.

Felicia stammered, "Second, *what*? Gene." She snapped her fingers. "Anna. Zoom in."

So Tuesday knew she was being filmed. Her mother and father would for sure see these images. Her old coworkers would watch as she kissed this man while wearing her wet black T-shirt, her butt hanging right out of the black panties that were smaller than a bathing suit, no question.

She didn't care.

Instead, she grinned.

Aidan swept his arms lazily through the water, closing the gap between them. "I figure we'll give them this one."

"Sure." Her voice was breathy.

"Because they won't get to film all of them."

Her knees literally buckled. She bobbed down into the water, up to her neck again. Aidan caught her like he had the last time (he seemed to be getting good at it), his arm around her back, his other hand hot against her cheek.

He kissed her.

A normal kiss. Closed lips. It should have made her feel good. Sexy, even.

Instead, it was so much more. It lit her entire body on fire, and it made her want so much impossibly more, so much more than she could possibly get from anyone, ever, least of all this man whose body seemed meant to hold her. The water shifted, rocking them both, and her right leg wound itself naturally around his left one. His lips danced over hers, kissing, nibbling, tasting. She breathed him in, and felt him grow hard against her.

Two scraps of fabric.

That was all that was between them.

She pulled a few inches away. Her voice was little more than a whisper, but she couldn't seem to find the air she needed for more volume. "How many people watch this show?"

He shook his head. "Dunno."

From behind them, Felicia yelled, "Two point three million watched the last episode."

"How..." Tuesday looked up. The fuzzy mic bounced above their heads. "I forgot about that."

Aidan drew her closer. "So I guess shouldn't tell you what I want to do with you."

There was even less air now. She prayed she wasn't gulping like a fish. "Can you hold that thought?"

"Oh, I'll hold it, all right." He skimmed the flat of his hand against her breast. She bit the inside of her lip. Even in the heated water, her nipple tightened.

Felicia called out again. "When's your first date?"

"Tonight!" yelled Aidan with a laugh.

Tonight? That was too soon. She wasn't...ready. She needed more time. This man scared her somehow.

No, he didn't scare her.

He was the opposite of scary. He was intense, but not frightening.

He was making her scared of *herself*. "Not tonight."

Aidan lowered his gaze to hers. Both of his hands were at her waist, and he moved his hips so his rigidity wasn't pressing into her. "Tomorrow?"

"Okay. Sure." The smile kept creeping onto her face. She was equal parts freaked out and turned on, and she had *no* idea what to do about it.

"She said yes to tomorrow!" Aidan called over her shoulder at Felicia.

Felicia shot a thumbs up. "What are you going to do?"

Aidan yelled cheerfully, "Hang gliding!"

"Oh, shit." Tuesday clapped her hand over her mouth.

"Don't worry!" Felicia yelled. "We'll beep that out!"

CHAPTER TWENTY

The next day, even though she was standing on solid earth (for now), Tuesday was still kicking herself for not saying no.

She *should* have said no.

Not to the date—she very much wanted to spend time with Aidan. Too much so, perhaps.

But the very second Aidan brought up *hanging* from a *glider* (two words that shouldn't really go together), she should have shot the idea right out of the sky.

No. No way.

Instead, she'd probably end up being the one who needed to be shot out of the sky when she went too high into it. Or scraped from the pavement when she hit it. Or rescued from the ocean when she plunged into it.

What if something she did brought both of them down? *What if he got hurt because of her?*

Lord have mercy. She wasn't ready for this.

"Look." Aidan pointed over the edge of the cliff. "Perfect conditions."

Tuesday wrapped her arms around herself and shivered. "To die? Is that what you mean? Because perfect conditions to me are when I'm sitting in front of a fireplace, reading a book."

They had one camera pointed at them—Gene was lazily filming and sipping his coffee at the same time—but the others were building establishing shots, Felicia had said. They had plenty to film, that was for sure. According to Google, Pine Tar Bluff was one of the state's most popular hang gliding launch points. There were at least twenty people in the air already, all of them hanging from what appeared to be short sleeping bags. Sometimes the fliers drifted overhead and called down to the people they knew on the ground.

Aidan seemed to know everyone. How he was getting anything done with the amount of waving he was doing to everyone and their dogs? Seriously, there were *so* many dogs. As well as being a hang gliding park, it was also an off-leash dog park, and Tuesday had never seen so many dogs running happily in one place.

It was dog paradise.

It was probably hang-gliding paradise.

And four people had died here in the last fifteen years.

Tuesday really shouldn't have googled.

"How are you doing?"

"Me? Oh. Panicking."

He laughed as if she were kidding, and kept working on the metal hooks that were part of the long metal bars he'd assembled in front of him. Then he glanced up at her. "Oh, you're serious. You'll be fine."

Tuesday was grateful that she hadn't eaten. There's no way she'd be able to keep anything down as soon as they rose into the air.

"I don't think I know enough."

"You know everything you need to." Aidan had spent an hour telling her exactly how the hang gliders worked. It had seemed an equal combination of aeronautics education and pep talk. "You're going to be just fine. You'll be with me."

Did that make it better? Or did that actually make it more terrifying?

Tuesday wasn't sure.

On the one hand, she was grateful she didn't have to make any kind of solo flight. She had no interest in that whatsoever. If she flew solo, she'd be responsible for all the people on the ground she could hurt if she crashed.

On the other hand, that meant she'd be strapped to the man currently kneeling on the ground in front of her. Tandem gliding meant he'd hold her in front of him in her own little half-sleeping bag. Their bodies would be pressed together in the air.

"What if I pass out?"

"Up there?"

"No." Tuesday sat down on the wind-blown brown grass next to him. "Right now."

"I don't mind."

"Big of you."

"Better for you to get that over with beforehand. That's all I mean."

Tuesday decided to try a different angle. "Did you know one in a thousand people die hang gliding?"

"Nice try."

"It's true!"

"I know, but that stat is for regular flyers. Did you read that, too?"

"Yes," she admitted.

"Not for students or for people who fly tandem. When you add all those hundred of thousands of people in, the stat goes way down."

Tuesday rubbed her palms together. "I think that makes it worse. Don't you think? That the rate is higher for regular fliers?"

He smiled at her, and for the first time all morning, Tuesday felt warm. "You'll be fine. We'll be fine. And we're about ready."

Anna was running the show this morning instead of Felicia. "Cam two and three, round up," she said into a headset. Was Felicia home? With Liam? Was she having more morning sickness?

Should she really do this?

Should she run?

Tuesday curled her toes in her shoes, the way her therapist had told her would help.

So she'd had a traumatic accident. So the doctor said she had a touch of PTSD. "I can do this."

"You can totally do this." Aidan lifted the suddenly put-together glider and shook it by the metal triangle, as if to test it for something. "You ready?"

"No."

He grinned at her, and the smile made her believe that maybe she wouldn't die today.

"Okay. I'll try."

"Good girl."

Girl. Sheesh. She scowled. "What's Jake doing right now, you think?"

"He got the all-clear from the doc. He should be at your house right now, working with the guys on taking down those bathroom walls and cutting in geothermal pipe from the street."

"Sounds wonderful. What a guy."

"You want to switch back to him?" Aidan's smile was something else. It said *We're smiling together, you and me.* Did anyone *not* fall for it?

"Probably. If I don't die, I expect that's what I'll do."

Cheerfully, Aidan said, "Figured you would. Good thing I'll get in a flight first. Now come on, you. Stand with me and we'll get your harness on."

Gene ducked under the wing to get one more close up of her face. On the other side, Anna adjusted the GoPro cameras attached to both of their helmets.

Ten minutes later, they ran off the edge of the cliff.

Okay, it was really more like a hill. But it was a *steep* hill. She kept her eyes up, as instructed, though it felt completely counterintuitive. She'd never run down a hill without watching her feet. Behind her, Aidan ran, too. Both of his hands were outside hers on the control bar. Above her head, Tuesday could hear the nylon creaking against the rigging.

"Legs up!"

The wind strengthened, and her harness tightened automatically as they were tugged upward.

"I can't." He wouldn't be able to hear her, not with all the noise around them, the roar of the wind, and the flapping of the nylon.

But somehow he did. "I'm right here."

So she lifted her feet as he lifted his, and just like that, they were free.

They were in the air and suddenly, it was so much quieter. They were *with* the wind, instead of battling it to stay on the ground.

Tuesday's stomach fell away and stayed away, which was fine—she didn't need it. She was too busy trying to handle the drunken happiness that filled her as surely as if her blood had been replaced by wine. Really, it was like standing still as the world dropped below them. Instead of flying up, she felt as if the ground was falling away—instead of them veering to the right, the earth sailed to the left.

"Trust me." His voice was a rumble in her ear, muffled through the helmet but perfectly clear.

Something about the way he said it made her spine relax, her neck lengthen. She'd been holding a ball of tension tightly between her shoulder blades, as if by sheer force of will she could keep the glider aloft.

Tuesday tried relaxing her muscles, ready to clench again if she had to.

But she didn't have to.

She was in the circle of Aidan's arms, her hands on the control bar with his. His body pressed against hers, a happy, heavy weight. She wasn't tethered to the earth anymore but she was tethered to him, and that was better than anything she'd expected.

Her eyesight grew sharp as a falcon's, even through the safety goggles fitted over her glasses. They soared over the ocean, and instead of being certain of the drowning that was in her very near future, Tuesday was able to focus on the small white sailboat below. A man was on deck, a fishing pole in his hands. He wore sunglasses. Tuesday could almost read the writing on his shirt. "Hello!" she called downward.

The man waved, and Tuesday whooped.

She could fly.

Why was she so surprised? After all, when she was young, flight had been her dearest dream, her favorite imaginary superpower.

She felt, rather than heard, Aidan laughing behind her. They should fish, from up here. They could drop a net, and Aidan could steer as she trawled, and then they'd fly over Darling Bay, her arms full of fresh-caught fish still flapping. She could imagine the looks on people's faces, as they gazed up to see the hang-gliding fishers.

The laughter didn't stop. It bubbled up, filling her lungs with joy. Every time Aidan caught a thermal updraft, she giggled. As they soared, banking over the sand, she laughed more. She was carbonated, her blood full of something fizzy that she couldn't control.

Aidan said, "Take the control bar."

"Me? No."

He moved his hands over so hers could take his place. "Use your body. Just shift your weight."

"I can't." She'd crash this thing. She couldn't even drive a car anymore—too many other people on the road. She couldn't *fly*. She couldn't hold a man up in the sky.

"You don't have to do anything but hold the bar. Shift your weight when I tell you."

"Aidan—"

He took his hands off the bar.

Just like that, Tuesday was driving.

They didn't hurtle toward the ground. They stayed up. They went higher, in fact.

Something loosened in Tuesday's chest.

How far could they go? Did they actually have to land? Was there a way to get food and water delivered up here? Could they stay forever in the sky like this? Tuesday's face and hands were cold but she didn't mind.

No, Tuesday was *flying*.

"Good," he said. "Good job."

Aidan was the reason she could fly. She shimmied against him in joy, and she felt him respond.

For one split second, she wondered if anyone had ever had sex while hang gliding. It seemed impossible, and they were in different harnesses, but then again, people who wanted to have sex in strange places usually managed to get it done. Just imagining it made Tuesday overheat like she'd forgotten to fill her own personal radiator. She wondered if Aidan could feel it—the flush that took over her body.

A sudden gust of wind made the control bar buck. Fear rolled through her. She was driving this thing—she could crash it if she wasn't careful. "Take it back?" she called to him. "Please take it back." Her voice shook. She hoped he didn't hear it.

But he just took the bar back and said, "Ready for your surprise?"

The dirty image that filled her mind shocked her. "Yes," she called back to him, grateful he couldn't see her face.

"We're escaping."

"What?"

"First, let's do a fly-over." Aidan steered them back over the spot from which they'd taken off. The camera crews obediently faced their lenses up, and Tuesday laughed down at them. She waved. Gene and Anna waved back. "Are you having fun?" she heard someone call, and another laugh was the only answer she could manage.

"Now, we get out of here."

Out of here? They were supposed to land in the same field they'd taken off from. If they didn't, where would they land? How would the network van know where to follow them?

Oh.

Maybe Aidan didn't want the network van to follow them at all.

More warmth suffused her, this time heating her face. The cool salt air hitting it was a relief.

They soared north, dipping down and then raising back up again as he caught the updrafts. She knew they couldn't go much inland, or they'd lose the coastal thermals, but maybe he was taking her to a different beach?

It wasn't until she spotted the Callahan house—*her* house—that she realized where he was heading. "They'll find us," she called.

"Not for a little while," he said, banking left toward an empty field. "Remember what I said about keeping your feet bent until mine are on the earth? I'll stop us."

She swallowed her terror and held her breath.

The landing was both worse than she'd thought it would be—the earth moved under them much faster than she'd thought it would—and easier, too. She just stood up when the motion ceased.

Tuesday laughed in sheer delight. Her cheeks felt windburned.

Aidan helped them disentangle, first her, then him. He reached forward and took off the camera attached to her helmet and turned it off. He did the same to his camera.

He turned to her. "Now. We're off the radar and we can do one of two things." His eyes were lit from inside, a heat that she wanted to press herself against even though she was still overly warm from the excitement of coming down.

Tuesday raised a finger. "Tell me one."

"We call Anna and tell her where we are. They come get us, film us some more, and maybe we go get a sandwich or a meal somewhere."

In response, Tuesday's stomach growled. She put up another finger. "Tell me option two."

Aidan pointed to a low line of bushes that ran along the deserted one-lane road. "We pull out the bicycles I hid in those bushes this morning. We ride them to your hot spring. We soak and then have a picnic."

Joy rose through her, pushing against her as the wind had. "You have *food*?"

"Oh, yeah."

Impulsively, Tuesday pressed her hands against his chest, lifted up on her tiptoes, and planted a close-mouthed kiss against his lips. "You're a genius. Let's go." Her voice came out surprisingly breathy, and she swayed backward, away from him. Had he moved toward her? Or was that her imagination?

Aidan cleared his throat. "Yeah. Yeah, okay. Let me text Anna where I'm leaving the glider." He grinned at his phone. "The biggest problem with this thing is transporting it to and from, and I'm going to make them do the second half."

"They must think we crashed and died somewhere."

"Nah, they'll have seen the footage from our helmet cams until I turned them off. If Anna asks Jake or Liam about it, they'll know we went into hiding. But yeah, I don't want them to worry too much."

Into hiding.

It sounded illicit.

Tuesday was all in.

CHAPTER TWENTY-ONE

T uesday was a good, strong bike rider. He should have known, with those incredible calves. As they came around the Third Street curve, she grinned at him, looking cute as hell in her red hang gliding helmet that had doubled nicely as a bike helmet. "They're probably freaking out right now."

Aidan had no doubt they were. He was going to hear about this for the rest of his life from Felicia, and he was glad she hadn't come in this morning. "Probably. But right now, we've got some time."

They hid the bikes in an alley four houses down from the Callahan place. He shouldered the picnic backpack and put the blanket over his arm. "I know a shortcut through the Hildeboom's backyard. Come on."

Then they were in her yard, ducking low, hoping none of the workers looked outside. Tuesday giggled behind him, and the sound sent a shiver up Aidan's spine. He pushed open the gate, shoving the cut wisteria branches and vines out of his way, praying that she was in the mood to get down to her underwear again.

Or less.

He held the gate open for her. "Ladies first."

She slanted a look he couldn't decipher at him and ducked under his arm. "You don't have any water on you, do you?"

Aidan gestured at the pool of steaming hot water. "Like this?"

She shook her head. "Never mind, I'm fine."

"Or do you mean like this?" He pulled a bottle of water out of the backpack.

"You're magical."

Damn it all, her smile was so *sweet*. How was it that a woman who looked like she did—like the grade-school teacher she was—could light him on fire like she did? He cocked his head to the side and watched her as she drank. She was unselfconscious, glugging it down. She saved the last half for him.

"Here you go. Thank you. You probably saved my life." She shivered.

"You cold?" He felt a shiver, too, low in his torso.

She nodded. "I think it's just the excitement of landing. I can't stop shaking."

"I get that way sometimes."

"You do?"

He did, though it was usually only when he had a hang gliding call that felt too close. A few months back, he'd swooped so close to the edge of the cliff he felt the wing tip scrape the very edge of the rock. A little harder, and his flight would have been abruptly ended—he would have fallen to the hard-packed sand fifty feet below. He'd shook like she was now.

That didn't explain why he was shaking at this moment, though. It was almost imperceptible—when he sneaked a look at his hand, he couldn't see the tremors.

But he could feel them.

They were entirely due to Tuesday.

Tuesday.

"Let's do this," he said.

Aidan went in first. It was only sensible this time. Once Tuesday stripped down to her underwear, he'd be hard again, and if he was in the water, it would be a secret.

And he would get to watch.

Tuesday stood on a wide, mossy rock and pulled her pants off first. She folded them carefully. She paused, as if thinking.

She took off her glasses. "I'm putting them here, on this stump." She pointed. "So later, when I'm panicking, you'll be able to tell me where they are."

"Can you see anything without them?"

"Nothing far away, but I can see okay up close."

He'd have to stay close to her, then.

Another pause. Then Tuesday stripped off her shirt.

She had a scar. *Damn.* A big one, thick and angrily red. The viciousness of it took his breath away. The scar snaked from under her right breast, across her stomach, and into the top of her panties.

She caught him looking, and her face flushed. Her cheeks went so pink he forgot to think about her scar and whether she was okay. He could only think about how damn hot she was.

"Tuesday—" He took a step through the water toward her. Then another.

For a long moment, her gaze met his. Something smoldered between them—a bomb's wick, lit and running fast.

Then she smiled, and dove forward. She stood for a brief second, the water up to her armpits. Then she closed her nose with her fingers, and dropped below the water.

It broke the spell, as she'd probably meant it to. Aidan shook his hair, spraying droplets everywhere. He felt *alive*. He was fully inside his body, and he felt every breath of wind, heard every low creak in the treetops that ringed the pool. Far off, a dog barked, and then another one joined it. Aidan thought for a second about joining their joyful howling.

But he was waiting for Tuesday to reappear.

Three more long seconds.

Then three more.

Jesus.

How long was she going to hold her breath? Aidan shifted from one foot to the other. Had it been twenty seconds? Forty? Longer?

She was fine. It wasn't even four feet deep where she was.

There were no creatures waiting to bring her down. No Nessy in this hot spring (though one of the Homeless Petes had sworn he'd seen a lizard monster in the storm drain behind City Hall more than once).

There weren't even any big tree roots to catch her foot underneath the water—just flat, silty rock.

Three.

Two.

One.

That was it.

Aidan launched himself at the place he'd seen her last. His hands touched her body—maybe her shoulders?—and he grappled to get a grip on her arms. He hauled her up and out of the water, pulling him against himself.

"Oh!" Tuesday spluttered.

"Are you *okay?*"

She gave him the same smile she had right before she'd ducked under the water. "I like to see how long I can hold my breath."

Aidan's frozen blood start to move again. The heat of the water helped. So did the feeling of her body against his. "Next time, warm me."

"Do you mean *warn* you?" She tilted her head coquettishly. How had he possibly thought this woman was regular-looking?

He nodded. Yeah. That's what he'd meant to say. He opened his mouth to correct himself, but instead of speaking, he raised both his hands to her wet face. For a split second, her expression stilled. Sobered.

But her eyes still danced, and lord give a man a little mercy, she was irresistible.

He kissed her.

Or did she kiss him? It was impossible to tell. Her mouth tasted slightly salty, slightly alkaline. Her tongue was cool in comparison to her spring-heated skin. She pressed her breasts against his chest, and the two scraps of lace and his boxers that were between them did nothing to disguise her body from him. His hands roamed into her wet, tangled hair, down her dripping spine, to the curve of her ass. He cupped both her buttocks, and she moaned into his mouth. He bent his knees, sinking deeper into the water, and lifted her so that her legs went around his waist.

Tuesday put her hands on his chest and pushed herself a few inches away, leaving her legs wrapped around him. Aidan froze. He needed this woman on a cellular level, but if she said stop, of course he'd stop.

How he'd stop, he had no fucking clue.

But he would. "You okay?"

Her answer was to tilt her pelvis against his hips. She pressed herself lightly against his cock, and she looked as frustrated by the fabric between them as he felt, her eyebrows drawn together, her lips tight. "Um."

"Tuesday?"

"I'm okay," she choked.

"Really? Because—"

"I'm not okay."

Aidan opened his hands, releasing the grip he'd had on her hips. "All right—"

"I want more."

The words didn't make sense to his overheated brain. "Huh?"

"But I'm about to spontaneously combust. Can we get out?"

Stop. She wanted to stop. That was it. Fine. "Yeah. Yes, yeah." He stood slowly from kneeling, but her legs were still wrapped around his waist, and she made no move to release him. Pressing into his feet, he stood all the way up, holding her against him. The water made him unsteady, and he swayed.

He was still hard as a rock.

Nothing he could do about it, really. Not for a few minutes at least. He took a breath. Her mouth was an inch from his, their noses almost touching. Water sheeting from their bodies. "Getting out. You want to eat lunch?"

Tuesday bit her lower lip, as if she was considering something. "I want...Oh, God. I can't say what I want."

He could barely breathe. "Anything is—Tuesday, tell me. Yes or no."

"Yes," she whispered. "For fuck's sake, yes."

CHAPTER TWENTY-TWO

Aidan grinned, feeling like he could fly without the glider. "For the very sake of the fuck, then, follow me." She unwrapped her legs, and pushed against his chest lightly, putting her feet back into the water. Her took her hand. Without another word, he led her to the edge of the pool, then stepped up and out.

She was grace and beauty, water streaming from her strong limbs. Her scar didn't mar her body—it made her look stronger. Next to her, Aidan felt like a bumbling oaf. He stumbled as he stepped up onto the lowest rock.

He led her to the blanket in the shade. Carefully, he moved the picnic backpack onto the grass.

Tuesday sat. "I'm getting the blanket wet."

"Mmmm. Do I need to be careful here?" He touched the skin next to the scar on her stomach.

She shook her head wordlessly.

He didn't ask then. He took.

He covered her body with his, pressing her onto her back. He tried to keep his weight on his elbows as he kissed her, as he moved his mouth down her neck, as he played with the edge of her earlobe with his teeth. His arms shook, though, and she scooted sideways so that he could rest fully on one elbow. "Good," he said. "I can see you this way."

Tuesday closed her eyes as if she were going underwater again. Then she opened them and said. "See more of me, then."

Aidan's mouth went dry.

Fuck, yes.

He rolled onto his back and pulled her on top of him. He unclasped her sodden bra. It dropped to the blanket next to them, and Tuesday straddled him, her bare breasts tilted up toward the sun.

They were glorious breasts—full and round and surprisingly heavy. He curled himself upward, moving his mouth to take one nipple and suckle it before moving to the other one. He got harder, and when she moved her hips against his, he couldn't stand it anymore. He had to have her, and God help him, he had to have her soon. Before he died of this feeling.

He tugged her mouth down to his, and spoke against her lips. "I need you."

She gave a whimper that further served to rid him of conscious thought. She slid sideways and tugged off her panties before helping him with his wet boxers. Huh. He should feel cold, a small part of his brain said. There should be shrinkage.

Thank God, there was none.

There was the opposite. He reached down and felt his shaft, which had never been as hot or hard, perhaps in his whole life. "Wallet." He pointed at his jeans which lay next to the blanket.

She understood and complied, handing him his wallet. He extracted the condom stashed behind a couple of twenties.

"Did you only bring one?" That crooked little grin again, and Aidan exploded into action.

He ripped open the package. She tried to help him put it on, but there were three seconds of fumbling, and that kind of carelessness might actually kill him, and he had no interest in dying at the present moment—he only wanted to live, to live hard, preferably inside her, and preferably soon.

The condom was on.

He rolled her onto her back.

He held himself over her. "I feel compelled to point out that foreplay is a thing I'm usually better at."

"Are you kidding me? You made me *fly*."

CHAPTER TWENTY-THREE

Tuesday tilted her hips, and pressed her opening to the tip of his shaft, and with one fast stroke, he was inside her. She felt hotter than a furnace and he filled her so tightly, it almost hurt. She gasped a breath.

He made the same noise. She wrapped her arms around his waist, pulling him against her. "Wait." Her breath was a quick pant. "Just a second. Let me—you're big."

"We can stop."

They could. She might die, though, if they did, and if she'd lived through hang gliding, she could live through this.

So Tuesday growled in his ear. "*More.*"

He took her mouth, biting her lip as he ground his hips into hers, plunging again and again, each time a little deeper. She could feel herself get tighter and tighter.

He slid his hand between their bodies and pressed his thumb against her clit.

The pleasure was *too* big. Too intense. She gave a short scream, pulling her mouth away from his.

"Yes?" he asked.

"Fuck, yes. But here." She used her own hand to adjust the placement of his thumb and then—suddenly—bit the side of his neck to keep from screaming again.

Time slowed to a stop. Tuesday was aware of everything. Each time he pushed into her, she felt the shudder than ran through him. Her hips shook and trembled as she pushed her clit against his thumb. He let her drive the rhythm, matching his strokes to her shivers. She wrapped her free arm around his neck, and he buried his face in her hair and he fucked her so hard and so fast that her body exploded under his at the same time that he came so hard, so deep that she thought neither might ever stop coming. She clenched around his cock, again and again, spasms rocking her torso. A fine trembling started in her arms, and moved to her legs, and when he kissed her again, they panted against each other. She tasted sweat on the skin between his upper lip and nose, and the way he laughed, moving inside her as he did so, made her gasp.

"Holy shit." She held the side of his face in her hand. "Holy shit."

Aidan dropped to the right, sliding out of her, palming the spent condom as he did. "Holy shit," he agreed. "Are you okay?"

"No." She rolled to her side and propped her head on her hand so that she faced him. "I'm crazy. I feel literally crazy."

He nodded. "I feel like someone scooped out my brains and put them in a pan on the stove and then scrambled them, like they were eggs."

Her eyes widened. "That's it. Exactly." Sun poured over his shoulder.

He lifted a hand to touch the end of a strand. "Your hair is still dripping."

She grinned. "Not the only part of me."

He sucked in a breath.

Her stomach rumbled, loudly.

"Wow," Aidan said.

She pressed a fist against her naked skin. "Oh, my God, that sounded like an animal." Tuesday *felt* like an animal—a perfect beast, and she didn't need taming—she just wanted to be near him. For as long as possible.

"Good thing I brought provisions."

They sat up, wriggling a little self-consciously into their clothes.

But Tuesday wasn't ashamed or embarrassed.

She felt glorious, in fact.

The way Aidan had looked at her when he was inside her had made her feel like the most beautiful woman in the whole world.

Sure, maybe he'd been wearing sex goggles. That happened. Tuesday had been comfortable in her own body and in her own sexuality for long enough that it wasn't a surprise when sex felt good. She'd had enough partners to know what she liked and what she wanted.

She liked to be fucked hard, so that the pounding set up an answering pulse against her clit, so that her G-spot got stroked directly enough that when she came it was a full-body experience. Tuesday didn't mind teaching anyone what she liked. She'd been with a couple of men who took offense to her helpful suggestions, and that was fine—she didn't see them again.

Aidan got it in one try.

She'd moved his thumb once, and his eyes had lit up, as if he were thrilled to learn.

She ate a deviled egg and watched as Aidan ate one, too. He put the whole half egg in his mouth in one bite. He closed his eyes and turned his golden face to the sun and smiled.

The rest?

The pace? His rhythm? The sounds he made in her ear, the way she responded to him in kind?

A slice of fear wriggled under the skin at her wrists, and she took a quick sip of the second bottle of water.

Nothing was perfect.

Nothing.

The man had practically hated her, just the week before. Tuesday tried to keep herself from thinking it to herself, but it was too late.

"What is it?"

Had he seen the shadow that had floated across her mind? "Nothing."

"Too much paprika." He nodded as if he were agreeing with a critique she hadn't made. "I knew it. I got a new brand at the store, and I really think the holes are too wide at the top. A little paprika is good, but a lot is kind of like getting punched in the face—"

"*Why* were you mad that I bought the house?"

His eyes widened, and he coughed around the egg. Maybe she should have waited until he'd finished swallowing.

But she didn't take back the question. She waited.

He shrugged. "Dumb reason."

"Tell me?"

He tilted his head and looked at her, his eyes narrowed. "I'm honestly not sure if I should."

"Why not?"

"I have ulterior motives."

"Aren't those usually secret?"

He nodded. "That's the point. I don't think you're the one to talk to about this."

Diana, I like him too much. Way too much. Tuesday consciously unfolded her posture, the way she did when she was talking to angry parents on Back to School night. "I think I'm exactly the person to talk to."

"Why?"

"Because I see the way you look at the house." It struck her that it was similar to the way he looked at her. Like it was something he needed to keep breathing, at the same time like it was something he wanted to back away from slowly.

"How's that?"

"Like it holds a part of your soul."

CHAPTER TWENTY-FOUR

Aidan felt his throat close up. She was too close, striking at the truth of it. Tuesday was the wrong person to talk to about it.

Wasn't she the enemy?

She had been.

But did most people want to kiss their enemy to within an inch of her life? Did they want to watch her eyes crinkle in that smile that made him feel giddy? Did they want their enemy to laugh that belly laugh that had the power to brighten an entire city?

Tuesday kept her gaze on him. Her leg jiggled, but the rest of her stayed still. "You can tell me the truth, you know."

Funny—the idea literally hadn't occurred to him until that moment. He sat with it for a moment, turning it over in his mind.

What was the worst that could happen if she knew what he wanted? He wasn't going to get it anyway, he was pretty damn sure about that.

"It's stupid," he said.

"Try me."

"I wanted you to sell the house to me."

Her brows slammed together.

Yeah, *that* hadn't been a good idea.

But instead of yelling at him, or worse—running away, leaving him alone on the blanket—she said, "That's why you were trying to scare me off of Darling Bay. Why would I sell you the house?"

"Because I want it."

A smile crept onto her face, but it was wary now. "You forget I teach kids."

The implication was he was being a child. *I want it!* "I know. I told you it was stupid."

"I just want to understand where you're coming from." She put cool fingers on his wrist, and it felt strangely like a hug.

This woman threw him. "Are you saying you'd consider it? Selling to me?"

She bit her bottom lip and then said, "You mean after the show is all done?"

"Yeah." Idiotic hope rose before he could squash it back down. "After it's wrapped."

"It'll be worth more then."

It would take him his entire natural life to pay off. "Yep."

"And you realize I'm fixing it up. To my specifications. You realize there's no good reason for me to even consider doing that."

"Actually, *I'm* fixing it up. My brothers. My business. My crew."

She picked up a red-wrapped piece of cheese and rolled it in her fingers. "So do you want every house you renovate?"

Aidan shook his head. "Unsustainable business model."

"I can't argue with that."

A small brown bird lit at the edge of the blanket. It hopped its careful way nearer the picnic as if it had seen enough of them in its time to know what it was. The bird was plain. Just a robin. Brown wings, brown-red chest, brown legs.

It cocked its head to the side, and its glittering black eye sparkled at Aidan as if telling him a secret. *I'm beautiful. People don't see that. But I don't mind. I know I am.*

The bird pecked at a fallen cracker and took off, half of it in its beak.

"Nervy bird," said Tuesday.

"I like nervy birds." Aidan took a breath. "And nervy broads."

She smiled at that. "Is that what I am?"

"Big time."

"How so?"

"You moved here from the other side of the country. Alone. To buy a house in a small town where everyone knows everybody, but we don't know you."

She shrugged. "No big deal."

"Very big deal."

Tuesday unwrapped the cheese and took a small bite. "*Please* tell me why you want the house so badly. Did you used to live there or something?"

He barked a laugh. "No way."

"Then what?"

Aidan curved his spine and leaned backward on his elbows. He looked up into the Coulter pine overhead. Is that where the bird had gone? Was it up there enjoying its cracker and watching them flail? "I wanted to live there. When I was kid."

Tuesday took another bite of her cheese and waited. Her legs were crossed and both knees jiggled up and down but she didn't appear nervous.

Not like him. Stupid. This was dumb, that had she so much fucking stupid emotion about an old wish. "It was just a dumb thing I wished for a lot."

"Who lived in the Callahan house then?"

"Mrs. Brown. She was my third-grade teacher."

"Did you have a crush on her?" Tuesday smiled, as if she were joking, but Aidan thought carefully about it.

"Maybe? But I don't think so. If anything, I had a crush on her family."

Tuesday folded the plastic cheese wrapper and squeezed the wax casing into a ball. Then she moved forward to lay on her stomach, just inches away from him. She propped her head on her hand. "Tell me more."

Aidan folded his hands behind his head. Above him, the tree disappeared and he could *see* the interior of Mrs. Brown's dining room. "They had this table. This big old long wooden table. In my mind it could seat about thirty people, but realistically it was probably only a twelve-seater. The top of the table was scarred with drink rings and scratches. On one corner you could actually see the word "Caleb" where her son had written too hard on a school paper, the force of his pencil pushing into the wood. I ate at their house once a month, and I can still remember running my fingers along that. Wishing it was my name there. There were always placemats on the table, and to my mind that was the fanciest shit I'd ever seen. At home, me and my brothers ate in front of the TV. When I was little, it was my mom who put our SpaghettiOs in a bowl, and then later, it was our step-dad Bill, but it didn't usually get much fancier than that. Once, at Mrs. Brown's house, she served us beef wellington. It was the most amazing meal I'd ever seen—the meat, there was just so much of it, cooked inside the pastry. When I took a bite, it tasted like I thought a dinner in heaven might taste." He'd forgotten that moment, though now he could practically taste it, the crisp yet soft crust, the tender and salty meat.

"Why did you eat there every month?"

Aidan remembered the way Mrs. Brown would ask him at lunch, always on the first Friday of the month, as if she had it written in her calendar. *Do you have plans for dinner? Would you like to eat with us?*

As if an eight-year-old would have dinner plans that extended beyond hoping for food. "I think I was her charity case for the year."

"Or her favorite."

Surprised, he searched her face. "Really? Teachers have favorites?"

She laughed. "We're humans, too. Of course we do. I had a girl in my class last year that I considered adopting." She folded her lips as if she'd said too much.

"Seriously?"

"No. Not really. She had a family. Sometimes."

"Not a good family."

Tuesday, still lying on her stomach, dropped her chin to the blanket and wagged her head back and forth. "The worst."

"But you didn't."

"You can't just take the kids you want. It's called a felony."

"Those wacky Minnesota laws."

"Go figure. Anyway, so she would have you over for dinner."

He closed his eyes and there it was again, that table. "After a while, it felt like I fit in. Her oldest kid, Caleb—"

"The same one who carved his name into the end of the table."

"He didn't mean to. But yeah. He and I got to be friends. He was only a couple of years older than I was. Looking back, I bet Mrs. Brown made him do it, but he was always nice to me."

"How?"

Aidan loved the way she asked him questions. Her eyes were wide, her gaze pinned to his face. She listened as if the answer mattered to her. "He would play Battleship with me."

"Old school."

"Yeah. They had all the early video games, too, and we played a lot of those, and watched MTV and blew up marshmallows in the microwave. Once we were fooling around with yellow paint—I think we were helping his sister with a dollhouse. When no one was looking I painted my name under the tabletop, in front of where I usually sat."

"Did they ever know?"

Aidan didn't think so. He shook his head. "If they did, they never let on. It was like I just fit in there. What I remember best was playing Battleship. Sinking his ships, and howling when he sunk mine." They would play at the table, at Caleb's carved corner. Mrs. Brown served them hot chocolate, thick with more mini-marshmallows on top. She would ruffle Aidan's hair and kiss Caleb's head. Aidan would fantasize about her kissing his own head (she never did). "I wanted her to be my mother."

"What was your mother like?"

"She gave birth to me." He grinned like he was telling a joke, and in a way, he was. His mother had loved their father enough to have three babies with him. That was probably the best thing she'd done as a mother. "No, that's not fair. Sometimes she tried." His first memory was his mother screaming at his father about getting diapers for Jake. His father had come home with a carful of stolen

Pampers, and the deputy had been on the porch within an hour.

"But not hard enough."

"Nope. Almost never hard enough."

"I'm sorry."

It sounded as if she really, really was. Aidan felt something in his throat, a small tickle that grew into a small knot. "Not a big deal. She and my dad split up, and she married Bill Ballard. He adopted us, legally."

"What about your dad?"

Aidan shrugged, looking up into the boughs overhead. "He signed off on the paperwork. Even laughed as they shook hands—I was watching from a window. Easy. I've always wondered if Bill paid him off."

"That's a terrible thing to wonder."

"That's one way to look at it. Another way is that Bill loved us so much that he was willing to do anything to raise us."

"So he was a good man."

"The best." Bill had loved each one of them differently. When Liam was ten, Bill had bought him a scientific calculator, Liam's fondest desire. With Bill's help, Liam learned how to use all the extra and mysterious buttons. When Aidan turned ten, Bill had built him a private workshop in the backyard. It was just a small shed, but Bill had filled it with second-hand tools they'd scrounged together at the flea mart fifteen miles up the coast. When Jake turned ten, Bill had given him his first sailing lessons. "He made us into the men we are. I wish he could have—"

"What?"

Aidan consciously unclenched his teeth. "I wish he could have seen that I turned out okay."

"He was worried about you?"

"I guess." He'd overheard Bill talking to Liam once. *Aidan's the one I'm concerned about. He's the most like your father. If he's not careful, he'll end up in jail. Or worse.*

The memory still hurt, like an old, deep bruise. Bill hadn't expected much from him.

He'd been trying to prove himself to a dead man for years.

Tuesday's voice was soft. "What happened to your parents? Are they still alive?"

His mother had left Bill in the end, taking none of her kids with her. "She went back to my dad. Both of them were killed in a meth lab explosion."

"Oh, God."

"Yeah."

"So." She paused, rolling onto her back so that she lay next to him, gazing up into the tree limbs overhead. "Mrs. Brown was the perfect mother."

"With the perfect family."

"And you think if you have that house and fill it with kids, you'll finally have that life you wanted so much when you were ten."

It sounded stupid every time he thought it.

Strangely, though, it didn't sound *quite* as dumb when she said it.

No.

It sounded incredible.

He rolled to his side. Better to admire the view. He tugged up the edge of her shirt, and she let him. His fingers traced the soft skin at her side, careful to avoid the scar. "My parents lied a lot. The Browns didn't."

"What did your parents lie about?"

What *hadn't* they? "Everything. Whether we'd eat that night. Where we were going to be living the next month. What that smell was in the kitchen, and why we couldn't touch what was in their bowls and plastic tubing."

"God." She scrunched her face as if the sun had just blinded her. "I hate parents like that."

It felt good to hear. "Once my mom dropped us off at this new school, and she said she'd be back at the end of the day."

"Yeah?"

"It turned out to be a state home, and she didn't come back for six months. This was about a year before she met Bill."

She rolled her head to look at him. Aidan wanted to kiss her, but held himself in check. "That's awful."

"When she finally did come back, I yelled at her. I told her she'd lied, and she denied it." *You didn't come back at the end of the day!*

I did, too! I just didn't tell you what day it would be!

"Mr. and Mrs. Brown had rules. No lying was the number one rule. I saw Caleb tell a lie about where the mouse in the garage had come from, and they were silent.

They just waited for him to change his tune, to tell the truth."

"Where *had* the mouse come from?"

"He'd bought it at a pet store and tried to keep it as pet, but he didn't want to put it in a cage. He was so upset when it went into the wall."

She smiled again, and Aidan felt his heart thump harder than it had when he'd been inside her.

Those eyes—when they were behind her glasses, they were pretty. When they were naked and looking at him like that? They were bewitching.

He had a thought then.

A huge thought, a thought that completed the vague wish he'd felt when he'd kissed her the first time.

Once he'd had it, he couldn't stop having it again. And again.

A child. A girl, or a boy, it didn't matter. A child with those brown eyes, with her depth of expression.

With his long nose.

With her mouth.

With his hair.

With her ears.

"What are you staring at?" Tuesday smiled but she back down her shirt. "You're kind of freaking me out."

"I think I just heard my biological clock." God, it sounded even worse when he said it out loud.

And sure enough, she laughed. "Men have those? Can you hear it ticking?"

"Maybe. Do you hear yours?"

She shook her head. "We're not talking about me. This is about you. I've never heard a man say that. What does it sound like?"

Aidan took a breath and swallowed his mild embarrassment. "It's more like a tickle than a ticking. I look at kids in the grocery store and I imagine them with my ears. Or with their mother's mouth." He couldn't help looking at Tuesday's lips. "Just think of it—two people love each other so much—"

"You sound like a commercial for a sex education book."

He wouldn't rise to her teasing, though. He was completely serious. "Two people in love making another person in their likeness?"

"How godlike." Her tone was gently mocking.

"How fucking incredible."

Tuesday stared at him. "You're totally serious."

"Dead serious. I don't think there's anything more important a person can do than bear children and raise them to be good human beings, loved and safe."

"Oh."

Was her tone disappointed? Worried? He took another deep breath and then asked the question that was suddenly so important it hurt the back of his lungs to hold it in any longer. "Do you want kids?"

CHAPTER TWENTY-FIVE

H is eyes were so bright, so hopeful, that Tuesday couldn't bear to see the light in them dimmed. She wanted him to stay like this. She didn't mean to lie. It just came out. "Of course. I love kids."

The funny thing was that it didn't even feel like a lie. It was what she'd said for most of her life, after all. She had wanted kids. Desperately.

But now? It was just that—a lie. And he'd *just* talked about telling the truth... She should take it back—correct herself, right now.

The grin on his face stopped her. God, he looked so *happy.* "Of course you do. You're a teacher." He tangled his feet with hers, and suddenly their lower limbs were pressing against each other.

If that kept happening, only one thing would follow.

So she sat up. "Yep. Hey, do you think we should pack up and find the camera crew?"

"Probably." He nodded lazily, and a stray shaft of sunlight landed on his face. His stubble was lighter than his hair, almost blond against his tanned face. He'd put on his jeans when she'd tugged on her clothes, but he was still shirtless. Cords of muscle knotted at his bicep, at his shoulder.

"Roll over?"

Without asking why, he did.

She touched the falcon that soared across his shoulder blades, tracing the blue ink down along his spine.

"Why a falcon?"

"It's a replica of a falcon painted on the face of a clock Bill had."

He was so strong.

And beautiful.

Tuesday was neither.

God, he'd seen her scar—had *touched* it, every red ripple and disgusting ridge. She hunched as she tugged her shirt lower.

"Wait." He reached forward, the very tips of his fingers dipping under the hem of her shirt and brushing the scar where it disappeared into her jeans. "Tell me."

"Nah, that's okay." As if he'd offered her more water.

"Tuesday?" He sat up, too, his cut abs tightening as he did. Was there not an inch of fat *anywhere* on the man's body? "You can talk to me."

She could. That was the problem. She really did feel like she could talk to him, but that wasn't what she needed.

She needed a home.

She needed quiet.

She needed time.

To heal. To think. To mourn the loss she'd just lied to him about.

She'd made him think she could have children.

What a joke. "Let's just pack it up for the day."

He caught her hand and twisted his fingers lightly with hers. "I just admitted I had a crush on a whole family. I wanted to steal them as a whole. I want your house because of it. That's kind of messed up. Won't you tell me your secret?"

A blast of energy, sharp and prickly, ran from the top of her head right down to her toes. She *wanted* to tell him. "Put on your shirt, at least."

He grinned. "I'm distracting you?"

She wouldn't admit it. *Don't say it.* "Yes." Crap. But at least she was capable of telling him the truth still. About some things.

While Aidan pulled on his shirt, she put on her shoes. She tugged her hair back with the rubber band at her wrist, and she found her glasses, still perched carefully on the stump where she'd placed them.

With her glasses on, she felt stronger. And she could see farther than the two feet separating their bodies—the whole glen came into focus. The water sparkled, a brown bird hopped at the edge of a wide gray rock, and the eucalyptus bent and swayed as if the whole world were moving. The air smelled fresh and damp.

Hopeful.

Aidan crossed his legs and leaned forward. Without ceremony, he caught her chin in his hand, and kissed her. It was a satisfied kiss, and a happy one.

The kiss made her feel stronger.

"Go," he said. "Lay it on me."

She shrugged. "Just your every day run-of-the-mill car accident."

"What happened?"

"I took a right turn. I had the green light, and—" this was usually as far as she could get without crying, but this time the lump stayed low in her throat. "I didn't check to the left. A minivan blew the light, and whomped into my car." Her fault. She had the green, yeah. She'd been awarded the settlement, yes. But forever she'd know it was her fault for not simply turning her head to the left to check for traffic.

"Were you alone?"

He *would* be smart enough to ask that. "No." Now her voice broke, and she hated herself that much more violently.

"Who were you with?"

"Two kids from school. Identical twin girls."

"Oh, shit."

Yeah. Teachers weren't supposed to drive kids home. It was against every rule in the book, for good reason. For *this* reason. But Maddee and Maggee were the twin daughters of her best friend. Diana'd had the flu, a bad case with a high fever, and her husband was out of town. Tuesday had texted Diana. *I was going to bring you hot and sour soup. Want me to drive the girls home so you don't have to get out of bed?*

She'd done it before. Maddee and Maggee liked being in her small electric car. They liked how quiet it was, how you could barely hear it when it was running.

Until the minivan crashed into them.

It had been the loudest thing Tuesday had ever heard in her life.

"Were they okay?"

She shook her head. "No."

"*Tuesday.*"

She liked the way he said her name. As if he wanted to fix something about the situation. If only he could. "No one died, don't worry." Sometimes she wished she had. "But Maddee's spine was broken. She'll be in a wheelchair for the rest of her life. And Maggee's face was slashed by a spring in the seat in front of her. Even though the surgeon was good—the best—her face will always be a little different."

He got it immediately. "Than her sister's face."

"Yeah." Diana's daughters would never be twins again. One would be low to the ground, wheels for legs. They didn't even have the comfort of having identical faces anymore. "They were the kind of twins who loved their twinship. Every day, they insisted on dressing the same. They loved fooling people."

"Did they ever fool you?"

Tuesday shook her head. "I was so proud of that. I think they loved me for it. I'd known them since they were

203

babies, of course, and I'd always been able to tell them apart. Something in the way they said their words. Maggee's voice was always just about half a pitch lower, and the way Maddee giggled was a little bit faster."

He closed his eyes for a moment. In horror? Was he wishing he were somewhere else? Then he opened them, and in his gaze was something that made Tuesday feel at once thoroughly warmed and at the same time completely terrified. "It was an accident."

How many times had she heard from her parents? "I know that."

"There's a saying about accidents. They happen."

Did he think he was going to fix this? Because nothing could. "It was an accident, I know. I hadn't planned on allowing the steering wheel to shred me internally. I didn't *mean* to maim my best friend's kids for life. But it was still my fault. I didn't look left."

"You can't let yourself think like that."

Oh, *really?* "I wasn't paying attention. And that's the thing—I'm the kind of person who *always* pays attention. To everything. But not that day. If I'd looked left when the light turned green, I wouldn't have pulled forward."

Aidan shook his head. "You might have anyway."

"*What?*" He didn't get to say that.

But apparently he thought he could. "We'll never know what might have happened if things were different. The minivan ran into you, right? That's like saying it's your fault that you left the school at the wrong time. If you'd just gone to the bathroom before you left, everything would be different."

She'd had to pee before she left the school, actually, but she'd been so intent on getting to the Chinese restaurant for soup and getting the girls home that she'd been planning to go at Diana's. Yeah, that made it her fault twice over.

Instead of stopping at the bathroom at school, she'd woken up in the hospital, tubes in her arms, to find EMTs cutting off her pants soaked with blood and urine.

"Enough." She stood.

"I'm sorry." Aidan jumped to his feet, too. "How are you and your best friend now?"

Tuesday laughed, but it sounded like paper crinkling in her throat. "We aren't."

"She won't talk to you?"

"Worse. She said she would." It had been a bottomless pit of pain. Diana's pinched white face, saying *It's okay. It was an accident. Of course I forgive you.* "I can't stop thinking that what she really wanted to say was that she couldn't forgive me, that I couldn't see her or the kids again. But it's Minnesota. You don't say that. We were practically family." God, it felt dumb to say out loud. It was the PTSD talking, that's what her therapist had said. Her therapist had said she needed to accept Diana's words for what they were, to not overanalyze them. Not martyr herself to what she *thought* Diana had been feeling.

Instead, Tuesday just kept writing the email that she would probably never send.

Aidan said, "So the only way out was out of town."

"Her kids would have been in my class in a year."

"Oh." Aidan winced.

"You know, I've been writing her an email for months? The longest email in the world, in which I say everything I would have told her if we were still talking. Sometimes I can't stop typing it. I stay up too late writing, and writing more is the first thing I do when I wake up. It's in my Drafts folder." *I told her about you. I told her everything.*

"I bet that hurts."

It felt good to to hear that. "Yeah. But less than not talking to her at all."

"What if...never mind."

"What?"

"What if she really did forgive you? What if she wants to talk to you, too?"

Tuesday shook her head. "No."

"I'm sure you've had all these thoughts. You don't need my input."

"Anyway," she said brightly, "that's where the blood money came from. The other driver's insurance paid for everything, a couple of million for each kid, and I got almost a million. Enough to buy this old house and start over."

He looked jarred, his jaw tightening. Was he disgusted by where her money came from? But he only said, "At its base level, though, it was just an accident."

An accident she'd caused. Nausea rose in her windpipe. "I know. In my heart I know that. It's just—how could she explain this to him? "I've spent my life watching out for things. Paying attention. But then I missed that car coming. I was driving the car in which the kids I loved got hurt. I've been trying to work through it—to get to a place of forgiveness, I guess—but then every time I do, I hear something loud that trips my brain right back into the feeling. Or I smell the burning plastic scent that blew into the car when the firefighters cut the door off."

"PTSD."

Tuesday shook her head, frustrated with herself. "Yeah. I've got a shrink and everything. Or I had one, anyway. I've got workbooks and journaling prompts. I've got support. But instead of getting better, I cut off my best friend and ran away."

"What if you just call her? Or text her?"

That was the thing, everyone had good, easy solutions. But no one else lived in her body. No one else felt the panic creep up her throat, they couldn't see the blackness that slipped in front of her eyes. "I know. I want to fix it, to fix us, but first I have to fix myself."

"How?"

Tuesday felt tears spring up behind her eyes, and she couldn't—she just couldn't do this. She would figure it out. Somehow. She *had* to. "I—oh, God. Do you mind if...? I'm going up to the house." The sounds of hammering had been filtering down the hill the whole time they'd been in the spring area. There would surely be someone on the crew, either construction or camera, who could take her back to the Cat's Claw. Later. When she'd finished shaking.

She was fast on her feet, and she left his voice calling behind her.

The gate slammed behind her. It sounded like something falling out of the sky, and she only barely kept her whole body from flying apart.

CHAPTER TWENTY-SIX

Felicia was standing on the back deck as Tuesday walked up through the overgrown garden.

"*There* you are. Oh, my God." Felicia rushed down the steps. "Are you okay?"

At least Aidan hadn't asked her that, hadn't said what she'd been *sure* he was going to say, *What about you? What about your scar? Were you hurt inside anywhere?*

People didn't usually ask this. They didn't want to know. Not when faced with the red rigidity of her scar. She'd learned that over the summer, the one time she'd gone to the beach with her parents. There on the shore of Lake Superior, she'd watched people first wince, then gird themselves, then smile up into her eyes cheerfully. As if it were nothing but a tattoo, not worthy of mention.

It had been awful.

She hadn't *wanted* them to mention anything. Yet she had. When people said nothing at all, it felt like a lie. A huge one.

Like the lie she'd kind of told Aidan when she said she wanted kids. She was an *idiot*. There probably wasn't therapy in the whole world that could help with that.

Felicia was still staring at her expectantly.

"We're fine. We landed and then went for a swim."

"Anna, I've got them back at the house." Felicia spoke into a walkie-talkie.

"*Copy.*"

"And you're okay?" Felicia was still looking her up and down. She craned her neck to look behind her. Aidan was just coming up the hill, taking long strides, the backpack over his shoulder and the blanket draped around his neck. "You guys had a date? Off camera?"

"The revolution will not be televised."

Felicia threw her arms up in the air. "That's the whole *point*. It *has* to be televised. I thought you'd both crashed and died!"

Aidan was close enough now to interrupt. "You did not. We had the cams on when we landed."

Felicia put her hands on her hips. "Okay. But. You owe me."

Anna came running around the side of the house, camera in hand. The sound guy was right behind her.

Aidan said, "Okay, to make it up for you, what do you want?"

"No, Aidan." Tuesday shook her head. "It's fine."

Felicia, though, nodded emphatically. "A kiss. A *good* one."

Tuesday winced. As if there was any other kind of kiss with this man. "Seriously?"

"I just made her run away from me. I guess kissing me isn't the best idea."

No, she'd run away from herself. "It's not the worst idea."

"Oh! Well, okay!" There was a sweet, funny lilt in his last word, and his eyes darkened as he set the backpack down on the ground and stood in front of her.

He smiled into her eyes. Tuesday forgot the camera, forgot Felicia was practically rubbing her hands together in glee.

With one strong hand, Aidan tilted her chin.

He leaned down.

Before he could kiss her, Tuesday sprang upward, on tiptoe. She planted a very swift kiss on his lips, before dropping back down to her heels again. "There," she started to say, turning—

Aidan caught her, first by one hand, then the other. He pulled her against him, threading her arms around his waist, and his mouth was on hers. She lost her breath and she was pretty sure that all the oxygen had left the atmosphere because she sure as hell couldn't find any. His mouth was hot, and it was life, and the way he tasted made her feel as if she'd never get enough of him—he was exactly what she needed, and the more she took of the kiss, the more she wanted. The world fell away like it had when they'd lifted off, hours before, and there was nothing but this kiss, this man, this moment.

He drew away, and she sighed, wobbling forward. She had to balance herself on his chest, and he smiled down into her eyes.

Oh, God.

She had it bad.

In the far distance, she heard a happy laugh, and when she turned her head, Felicia was clapping in delight. "Yes, yes, yes. You got that, Anna?"

Anna's own cheeks were pink. "I did. I think the camera lens fogged up, though, so we might have to do it again."

Tuesday's cell rang in her pocket. She pulled it out. "Crap. It's my mother." Tuesday moved away to answer. "I'm here."

"Where's here, darling?"

The group tromped into the house, and Tuesday made her way up to the porch, her knees feeling loose and hot, as if she'd been drinking. She sat on the top step. "At my new house."

Her mom made a small exclamation. "She's at the house, Ron!"

"Tell her to send us a picture!"

"Daddy says to send us—"

"Didn't you get the dozens of pictures I sent you on Facebook?"

"Well, yes. Ron, we have some."

"Send more!"

Her mother's voice got stronger. "How's it going with the young man?"

"Good."

"*Good* good?"

There was such hope in her mother's tone. Tuesday's heart ached like it had been nicked by a small, sharp knife. "Just okay good."

"Really? Did you throw up on his boat, lovey? You know it's okay if you did—remember what happened to you when we went sailing when you were five? Did you, honey?"

It took a second for Tuesday to track what her mother was thinking. "Oh! No. I'm dating Aidan now."

"You *are*? I *knew* it. I knew he was the man for you. Ron, she's dating Aidan now!"

"The big guy?"

"Mom, can you just talk to me right now? You can talk to Daddy anytime. I want to talk to you." The last few words came out in a pathetic whine, and Tuesday was irritated with herself.

"Of course. Honey, of course." A bang could be heard over the phone, and Tuesday knew without asking that her mother had moved out onto her own porch. The creak of the glider was next. "Tell me what's going on."

"Mom..." Tears welled, and her voice thickened with salt.

"What is it? You want to come home? You can come home."

If only her mother would just listen. "I think I'm falling for him." As soon as the words were out, they hung in the air in front of her, so real she could almost touch them.

They were true.

"Oh. Oh, honey. That's so good."

"No, it's not."

"Why not? Does he drink?"

"I don't know—"

"Is it drugs? Because all sorts of people are on opiates now. I saw it on a docudrama the other night. Heroin is the thing you have to watch for with people getting off of Norco. And Aidan works hard, I bet he's hurt himself in his job before—is it heroin?"

"Mom, just stop for a second."

"Okay. But—no, okay."

"He wants kids."

An indrawn breath, and Tuesday could almost see her mother's fingers tapping at her upper lip. "Oh."

"Yeah."

"Surely you're not there yet. Talking about *children*. You're just dating."

"I would have thought so. But there's something about this man..." There was something about Aidan that made Tuesday want to throw caution to the winds. Her best friend Diana had been single her entire adult life, not falling in love even once, but when she'd seen Nicholas, she'd known instantly that he was the man for her.

The man she'd have babies with.

Babies who'd turned into Maddee and Maggee. Babies who'd turned into children that Tuesday had injured, irrevocably.

"I think he's the one." Another partial lie. She didn't think it. She *knew* it. Deep in her bones, she knew it.

Her mother took a breath, but didn't yell it to Tuesday's father. Thank God. "Really, honey?"

"What about the baby thing?"

A pause. "Well, surely he'll be fine with adoption."

Despair felt black as tar in the pit of Tuesday's stomach. "He wants them to look like him."

"Surrogacy. Remember, the doctor talked about that?"

"No, like, he said he wants his kids to have their mother's mouth."

Her mother's voice grew brisk. "Well, he just doesn't get a say in that, that's all I'd like to tell *him*."

And that's why it was good this was all happening so far from home. "Thanks, Mom."

"You sound like you're getting a headache. Are you getting a headache?"

Tuesday hadn't been, but the more she thought about it, the better it sounded. "Yeah, I think I am."

Maybe a good old-fashioned headache would drown out the pounding in her blood.

CHAPTER TWENTY-SEVEN

The next morning, Aidan tried out the words in the kitchen of the Callahan house. "I'm falling in love with her." He wanted to see if they sounded out loud anything like they sounded in his head.

Jake barked a laugh and dropped a box of nails on the sawdust-covered floor.

Socal gave girly squeal and then laughed so hard she choked on her bagel.

"Fuck you guys."

Jake punched him in the shoulder, which hurt. "You've known her for two weeks. You've been on one date. Today. And I should point out that I've been on the same number of dates with her. You thought we *wouldn't* laugh at you?"

Aidan wouldn't give his younger brother the satisfaction of rubbing his shoulder. "I *thought* you would listen carefully and support my emotional needs."

Jake rubbed his eyes. "Oh, man, I wish Liam were here to witness this. This is the dumbest and best thing I've ever heard."

Aidan arched an eyebrow. "You forget, *On the Market* is how Liam and Felicia got together. Speak of the devil, here's the happy woman now."

Felicia entered the kitchen. "This is a disaster zone. Is it actually worse than yesterday? Is that possible?"

Aidan was so stupidly giddy he couldn't tell. It looked great to him.

Socal said, "Those cabinets we got at the salvage yard turned out to be full of dry rot."

Well, that would knock a guy's happiness right out from under him. Aidan frowned. "That sucks. What's your plan?"

"No big deal. The yard took them back, and Socal and I are going to run to Eureka this afternoon. We'll get something good."

Aidan took a breath.

Jake picked up on the hesitation. "Unless you don't trust us to go."

He didn't, not totally.

But if Aidan left the job site, then it decreased his chances of seeing Tuesday, and besides the damn cabinets and pipes and his lists and the million other things he should be thinking about, there was nothing else he could focus on.

Just Tuesday.

He'd gone by the Cat's Claw last night, after she'd left the site so abruptly, claiming a sudden headache.

Some headaches were the product of sunstroke, or dehydration. Was she sick? Did she need someone to take care of her? Would she tell him if she did?

He hadn't been surprised when Pearl Hawthorne had insisted on going upstairs to knock on her door for him. "This isn't a *bordello*, Mr. Ballard." Aidan was pretty damn sure she knew that it had been one, back in the 1890s, but it sounded like that maybe wasn't a feature in Pearl's eyes.

She come quickly down the stairs. "She's asleep."

"How do you know?"

Pearl hadn't thought this through. "Um. I mean, I guess she's asleep."

"Did she answer your knock?"

The more a person like Pearl got tangled in a lie, the worse they freaked out. "Um..."

"Because if she *said* to tell me she was asleep, she wanted you to lie on her account, right? What else is she lying about? Have you run her credit card? What if she's an international assassin, here to spy on the way Americans produce reality TV?"

Pearl's eyes were wide as the doll heads on the shelf behind her. "Oh!"

"I'm teasing. Did she say she had a headache?"

"Yes!" Pearl's relief was colored with the sound of truth. "She said she just wanted to sleep."

"Can you give her this? I know it's weird, but it helps my headaches sometimes." He passed over the ice cold orange Gatorade. "She was in the sun a lot today."

Pearl had smiled, promising to take it right upstairs, which, if he couldn't visit Tuesday, was as good as it got, he supposed.

Aidan had gone to bed, trying his best not to think of her. He'd managed the task for almost thirteen seconds, and then the image of her creamy breasts and those darkened nipples filled his brain. When he'd finally reached sleep, he continued to dream of her. In the dream, they sat in the Callahan house, eating dinner at the very table Caleb had carved his initial into, the tabletop Aidan had painted his name underneath in yellow. In the dream, Tuesday was just as beautiful—her hair a bit shorter, but warm brown. Her eyes twinkled behind her glasses. And her belly was round and high, her hands folded on top.

Aidan had woken with embarrassment that made him sticky with instant sweat.

He hardly knew Tuesday, but something in his very DNA recognized her.

He didn't have much interest in being anywhere that she wasn't.

And he hoped to God she might someday feel the same way because first, he wasn't a stalker, and second, it had been a long time since his heart had been broken, but he could guarantee that she would be able to do a number on his heart like no one ever had.

Now, in the kitchen with Jake and Socal and Felicia, three people he would literally trust with his life, he wanted to say it again.

"Yeah. I think I'm falling in love with her." He looked at Felicia, his new practice audience. If Aiden said it enough beforehand, maybe his voice wouldn't shake when he told Tuesday.

Felicia scowled. "*Shit.*"

"What?"

"No, I'm happy for you." She flapped a hand and pulled her walkie talkie off her hip. "It's just that I never see either of you coming, and I need a camera for this. Anna," she said into the mic. "Where are you? I need a diary cam in the kitchen."

Someone pushed Aidan across the floor until he was leaning against the wall next to the naked water standpipe. A woman swiped at his hair with a comb and a bottle of smelly spray, but he ducked the powder lady. Anna arrived, and perched a camera three feet in front of his face. Felicia stood to the side of it. "Look at me," she said. "Just have a conversation with me."

"With all these jackals around?" He gestured to his brother and Socal and half the camera crew. "How is this a diary anything?"

Felicia turned, shooing the rest out. "Go. Go! The bathroom upstairs—the skylight still isn't seated right. Go fix things! Anything." She turned back. "Okay. This is important. Forget that I'm here."

Nerves twitched at the base of Aidan's neck and he rubbed the top of his shoulder. "I thought I was supposed to be conversating with you."

"Conversating isn't a word."

He felt his eyebrows fly upward. "You're correcting me? On camera?"

"Future brother-in-law, I'll do a lot to protect you. But you have to trust me."

Irritation crawled along his skin. "But you just called me dumb."

"Is that what you think I did?"

"A big dumb blue-collar builder."

Felicia tilted her head, and her professional voice turned on. "Is that how you see yourself?"

"Only when people correct me about my English skills."

"It must be weird, then, dating a teacher. Are you self-conscious about your speech in front of her?"

Not until now. "No." But he dropped his eyes, and his voice was a mumble, and he *knew* how that would look on camera. Goddamnit.

"Tell me, then, in your own words, how you feel about the buyer of this house, Tuesday Willis. Please make the responses into full sentences."

Aidan glared.

"What?"

He pointed at the camera. "Ain't you gonna explain what a full sentence is to me?"

Felicia looked at him kindly. She waited.

Gah. This was probably going to be a mistake, but hell. What did he have to lose? The first time this played on TV, people would be able to tell how he felt about her. A long time ago, a girlfriend had warned him that poker wasn't his game.

Thinking about Tuesday?

Yeah, he could feel his face reacting.

Smiling.

"Tuesday Willis is incredible." He waited to see if that would be all that was needed.

"What about her strikes you as incredible?"

He thought. He kicked one boot over the other and rested a hand on the ungrouted tile of the new countertop. "The fact that she's doing this at all. Think about it. Would you be able to start over in a small town?"

Felicia drew her finger across her neck. "Talk to me, yes, but pretend I'm not here. And yes, I did start over in a small town. With your brother."

"Damn."

Felicia groaned. "Okay. Starting over. What's the most interesting thing about Tuesday to you?"

His heart sat up happily in his chest, a dog begging for a treat. "Everything. Everything Tuesday does and says is interesting to me. I think she could read me the card catalog at the library, and it would sound like the best book ever written."

Felicia smiled and made a go-on motion with her hands.

"There's just something about her—I want to get to know all of her. Have you seen her laugh? She lights up. Speaking of that, you should see her without glasses. She's model gorgeous. It's like maybe she hides herself in plain sight—she looks regular. Just a short girl with brown hair and brown eyes, right?" He could see her in his mind's eye. A brown robin. "And then she talks, and it's like the sun hits the top of her head with this golden crown, and her eyes sparkle like her soul is right there, in plain view, and she turns into the most..."

"The most what?"

Aidan looked down at his hands. "She turns into the most beautiful woman I've ever seen."

"Because of the light falling on her?"

He shook his head slowly. "It's because I see her for who she is. I guess it's like this: beautiful people walk around all over the place, and you get to know them, and then they get ordinary. Her, she's the opposite. She's normal until you get to know her and then she's like this supernova, all light and clarity and—" Aidan cut himself off. He was embarrassing himself again. "Jesus."

"Would you say you're...?"

It was easy to see what Felicia wanted. And it was even easier to give it to her. "Am I falling in love with her? Well, I thought I was."

Over Felicia's shoulder, he saw a person enter the dining area of the kitchen.

Tuesday. She was wearing a faded yellow T-shirt and ragged jeans. She curved at the breast and the hip. She had no makeup on, and her skin was a little paler than it had been yesterday. She looked as if she might still be fighting a headache, the space between her eyebrows pinched.

Aidan's mouth dried up. She was even prettier than he'd (repeatedly) imagined. He wanted nothing more in his whole life than to step away from the camera and kiss the hell out of her for the next three years or so.

Instead, he brought his eyes back to Felicia. "Sorry, what?"

"You said you thought you might be falling in love with Tuesday Willis, the buyer of the Callahan House."

"Yeah, But I was wrong."

Felicia stared. Behind her, Tuesday blinked, her eyes looking suddenly bruised.

"I was so wrong. I'm not *falling* in love with her. That time already came and went. I've done fallen. I'm in deep. I need one of those Darling Songbirds to write a song about the way I feel because my dumb words don't help what I want to say at all. But yeah." He looked directly at Felicia. He was too scared in the pit of his stomach to look past her at Tuesday. "I'm totally in love with Tuesday Willis, and America, I did *not* see this one coming."

Tuesday made a small noise, a cross between a squeak and a sneeze.

"So what are you going to do now about it?"

He had no idea. But he had a guess. "I'm gonna build her a house."

Tuesday had her fingers pressed to the top of her lip.

Aidan had a little more to say. "Did I mention what kind of house? Yeah. I'm going to build her the house of her dreams.

CHAPTER TWENTY-EIGHT

Tuesday had never worked harder physically in a long time, and certainly not since the accident. As she helped in the upstairs bathroom, laying tile, she nicked herself twice with the tile tool, and she couldn't stop sneezing from some kind of sealant the crew was using on the ceiling, putting in the new skylight.

Her back hurt.

Her fingers were killing her.

The headache she'd gone to bed with was still perched right between her eyeballs, as if it were waiting for her to let her guard down.

But she wouldn't do that. She *couldn't* let her guard down.

If she did, something insane would happen, like she'd walk back into the kitchen and find Aidan professing *love* for her.

Love.

She'd almost turned and run when she'd heard him say it to Felicia. It would have taken her ten seconds to be out of the house, and four hours to be at the airport, buying the first ticket back to Minnesota. She would leave everything she'd brought with her behind at the Cat's Claw. She didn't care.

But she always ran away.

At the same time, she'd almost run *at* him, too. That would have taken only five seconds, and most of that time would have been spent dodging Felicia and the camera guy. Tuesday could have jumped into Aidan's arms, knowing he'd catch her. She could have kissed him.

She could have told him she'd fallen in love with him, too.

Except that was crazy.

And God knew, Tuesday couldn't trust her emotions. Not since the crash.

Who fell in love with anyone on a first—albeit crazy and wild and awesome and scary and wonderful—date?

No one.

Except all the people who said they did.

Tuesday carefully laid another tile, cursing when it didn't sit the right way. Again. There was something she wasn't getting about tiling, and it didn't matter how many times Aidan showed her.

It didn't help that every time he put his fingers on hers, showing her the way to slide on the thin-set mortar and press down, she got the shivers, deep in her stomach. She felt redness suffuse her face, and when she'd stood to peek in the old vintage mirror she'd asked to keep, she looked like a tomato wearing a banana-colored shirt. She should teach pre-school, not fifth grade. She looked like a photo essay on primary colors.

She reached for another tile. Aidan kneeled next to her. This was all for the camera, of course—Tuesday didn't *have* to do a good job. The Ballard crew would take over and finish when Felicia got the shots of Tuesday she wanted.

"I'm all wrong for this," she whispered.

Aidan didn't hear her. "What?"

"Nothing."

Her parents fell in love with each other on their first date. It had always been both embarrassing and a point of pride for Tuesday. They'd gone out with a group to the movies, and had peeled off by themselves by the end of the night. Her father drove her mother home in his car and introduced himself to Margo's father as the man who would be asking for her hand as soon as he could save for a ring. They were married within three months, and Tuesday had come along ten months later. Ron and Margo still made out on the couch. Tuesday had hated that when she was thirteen. But it was that fact—knowing that her parents were truly happy together—that had allowed Tuesday to leave in search of a new life. If either of them had been unhappy, she might have stayed in Minnesota forever.

They'd been taking care of her so much this last year. After the accident, it had almost been full-time care for the first two months. It was high time not only for her to start a new life, but to give them an honest-to-God break from worrying about their daughter.

Her parents.

Diana and Nicholas.

People *did* fall in love at first sight.

But Tuesday had always known she wouldn't be one of those people. She was careful. She was thoughtful. She would *choose* when she fell in love. She wouldn't trip over it, like she'd tripped over Aidan the last time she'd tried to squeeze around him to get more tiles.

The room smelled of mortar and chalk. Out in the hallway, the air smelled of dust and plaster and old, newly uncovered dirt.

Aidan himself? He smelled like a pine forest. She didn't know if it was his deodorant or his shampoo—she didn't know if he was the kind of guy who splashed aftershave on his jaw. She only knew this: he smelled like something she wanted to wrap her legs around and climb.

That had to be the pine scent.

Right?

He'd tried conversation with her a couple of times, but she'd frozen up—her tongue felt tied with nervousness ever since she'd overheard him say he was in love with her.

On camera.

Who did that?

"Me, I guess."

Startled, she dropped yet another tile with a clatter. "Did I ask that out loud?"

He smiled, the right side of his rugged mouth tilting upward. "Unless I'm reading your mind, it was out loud."

God, imagine if he *were* reading her mind. Just like that, his clothes disappeared as she looked at him.

Her face went red hot.

Aidan said, "At some point we should talk about it."

"Talk about what?" Could she keep playing dumb forever? Sign her up. She was willing to give that a good college try.

"About the fact that I said I was in love with you."

Tuesday gave up the pretense of fiddling with the next tile. "Why *did* you say that?"

"Because I am." Aidan had been kneeling, but now he moved to sit with his back against the wall next to the tub.

"You can't be."

He held out his hand.

She wouldn't take it.

She wouldn't.

She would *not*—yeah, there her hand was. In his. Goddammit.

Traitorous hand. Did she have even a scrap control over herself at all? If this kept up, she'd be straddling his lap—

Yeah, it was her whole *body* that was traitorous.

She sat on his lap, her right knee on new tile, her left knee on the old wood. "I'll hurt the tile."

"You won't."

"I will."

"Then I'll fix it for you."

She sipped a breath of air. "I want the black enamel hardware."

Aidan shook his head. "The chrome is better."

"My house." She had to say it. "And I want the black enamel."

"But chrome is way better. It'll last longer. Never goes out of style."

"Black enamel." So far she'd been listening to him on the design choices. But it was her house. *Not* his.

"Hmmm." He looked amused, and it kind of pissed her off.

Only a little, though. It was hard to stay angry at him while sitting on his lap.

His eyes weren't just plain dark blue, she realized. They were deeper, like smoked cobalt. Bright blue cloaked in thick gray. His lips were an inch from hers, and she'd probably end up kissing him if she stayed here, but luckily she was going to die first because there was no way in hell she would remember how to breathe before she could get up and off him.

"Tuesday, are you okay?"

It broke the spell, and she sucked air into her lungs. "You can't be in love with me."

"A week ago, I would have agreed with you. Love at first sight doesn't exist. And then I saw you."

She snorted so loudly she bounced a little on his lap.

He winced. "Ow!"

"Not my fault."

He shifted slightly underneath her hips. "Actually, it is."

Warmth raced to her cheeks as she realized what he meant, but she managed, "That's the cheesiest line I've ever heard anyone say in my life. *Then I saw you?*"

He raised and lowered his shoulders, rubbing them against the wall. "Yeah, well. I didn't see it coming, either."

What was Tuesday supposed to say to that? She looked over her shoulder. Yeah, there was Anna and her camera, probably catching every word of it. At least Anna was far enough away she probably wouldn't be able to hear what they were saying until later, when they were going over the footage, pulling the audio from the mic packs Aidan and Tuesday wore.

When they played it on TV *nationally.*

Lord have mercy. "What am I supposed to do with you?"

"Let me take you out tonight."

"And do what?"

He arched an eyebrow and ran the back of his hand along the inner part of her arm. "I can think of a couple of things."

The heat in her torso grew hotter.

But she had a point, damn it. "I get it. We're attracted to each other. This—" she tapped his chest and then hers— "this is just lust. Comes and goes. I've felt it a million times before."

"A million?" He looked at her in mock horror. "Really?"

"You know what I mean. Lust is fun. We can have a good time. I'm not a prude." As the words left her mouth, she realized that only a prude would claim to be not a prude.

"Oooh, honey." He kept the stroking motion on her arm. Had the skin of her inner elbow ever been so sexually charged? "I like the sound of that, don't get me wrong. I, too, have lusted a million times. I've got no problem with acting on it, either."

No, he didn't. She knew that much.

"But I'm just saying, this is more. So much more. I'm in for the long haul."

What? Tuesday hadn't figured out how answer the kid question. That stupid lie—she had to tell him. Soon. She just hadn't figured it out yet. She was working on it...She scooted backward again. "Long haul?"

"You go any further back and you're going to break my kneecaps."

She couldn't do that. He had such sexy kneecaps. She moved to the side and sat on the tile, leaving her legs draped over his. "Long haul," she repeated. "Can I ask what your plan is?"

"Sure. It's easy. I'm just going to hang around until you fall in love with me back."

"Just to get a house?"

He didn't even blink. "I thought that was why. But I've inspected my heart, and that's not it."

"You can do that? Just lift out your heart and look at it?" Could he do that to hers if she asked?

"Sure. I know how to fix things."

"And if I don't fall in love back?" It was another lie of omission.

He shrugged. "I'm doomed. Already gone. I'll just enjoy it as much as possible."

That was it? "You make it sound so simple."

"I never thought it would be, honestly. I thought the idea of choosing one woman for the rest of my life would be pretty hard."

"And it's not?"

He shook his head slowly, back and forth. His eyes never left hers. He lifted a thumb and brushed it against her lower lip.

Tuesday could practically feel her eyes losing focus, her knees softening, her insides heating up again.

No. She was *not* going to have sex with this man in an unfinished corner of her new upstairs bathroom. On camera.

But hell.

She might complete the fall into love with him in that same corner. On camera.

Even with eyes wide open, she hadn't seen that coming at all.

She stood. "Black enamel hardware."

"Chrome is better," he called as she fled around the cameraman in the hall.

CHAPTER TWENTY-NINE

Tuesday was coming as unhinged as the door to the second bedroom that hadn't been fixed yet.

She made her way to the back porch and considered throwing herself down the hill, through the gate, and into the hot spring. But if she did, and he followed, then they'd end up making love again, and she would probably not let him leave her again. She'd have to become a true Californian and do some dryad ritual to make themselves into spring benefactors, and their fairy selves would cling to each other into eternity.

"Oh!" She pressed her hands to her cheeks in an effort to cool them down, but they felt as hot as her face.

"Boy trouble?" Felicia was sitting on the swing, her iPad in her lap, her notebook in her hand.

"I didn't even see you there."

Felicia shut the cover of her notebook. "I was hiding."

"I'm sorry, I'll leave you alone."

Sliding the iPad to the swing seat next to her, Felicia said, "No. Please don't go. Come sit with me. Off the record."

With a sigh, Tuesday lowered herself to the swing. "How are you feeling?"

Felicia looked startled, her eyes wide. "Um."

"I overheard you yesterday. I know you're pregnant."

"I guess I'm okay." She touched her stomach. "I'm just not used to the idea of it yet."

"But you're happy?" Tuesday wanted to take back the words as soon as they left her mouth. "I'm sorry, of course you are. That was so stupid."

"No, that's not stupid. I honestly don't know. I mean, I'm *happy*. But I'm way more terrified than I thought I would be."

Surprised, Tuesday said, "Really?"

"Yeah. I know that's not what people want to hear."

"What about Liam?"

"He's like me. Equal parts excited and terror." Felicia leaned forward, putting her elbows on her knees. "How does a person take entire, complete responsibility for another person?"

The faces of Maddee and Maggee flashed into Tuesday's mind. "I have no idea. Maybe they shouldn't."

It was a huge thought. What if a person *shouldn't* take complete responsibility of another person?

"You don't think I should have a baby?" Felicia looked startled.

"God, no! That's not what I meant. I only meant...Maybe you just have to accept you'll never *be* fully responsible for another person."

"But isn't that what a parent is?"

Tuesday would have thought so, once. "You can't protect them from everything, right? You can't stop an earthquake. Or a plane falling from the sky on top of your house."

"You are *really* freaking me out."

Oh, no, she hadn't meant to do that. "I only mean you can't control everything, so just concentrate on taking care of what you can. I bet you'll be a wonderful mother."

There was a pause. A small airplane whined high above mixed as a basketball was being somewhere down the street. The chain of the porch swing clanked quietly every time it moved forward.

Felicia pulled her bare feet underneath her. The way she looked at Tuesday—it wasn't like a person 'producing' her. It was more the look of a friend. "Enough about my neuroses. How are you doing, Tuesday? Off camera, like I said."

"I'm scared."

"Ahhh." Felicia's smiled stayed in place as her head tipped back. "I remember that feeling."

"You do?"

"I was terrified."

"You'd never been here before, either, right?"

Felicia nodded. "I only came as a scout. I was never supposed to be on the show."

"But you fell in love with that treehouse." It was her parents' favorite episode—the house with the enormous redwood tree growing up and through a two-story house.

"I did. And then the guy."

"How long—" She couldn't ask. She wouldn't.

"How long did it take to fall in love?"

Dumbly, Tuesday nodded.

"I walked into the kitchen at his office and saw the backs of his wrists moving as he slathered peanut butter on about a million sandwiches. I fell in love with him from behind. Before he'd said one word."

"See?" Tuesday groaned. "I appreciate what you're saying, I really do. But hyperbole isn't helping me here. When did you *actually* know?"

"All at once. After I'd lost him. That was the only time I knew I'd been in love with him since the first moment. It was like falling off a bed. You don't know you're doing it till you hit the floor."

"Oh."

"Yeah."

"So you can't really help me on this one."

Felicia laughed and patted her flat stomach. "You're not helping me with this, are you?"

"Not so much."

CHAPTER THIRTY

Tuesday looked down off the porch and saw Ella coming up toward them. Ella waved cheerfully. "Hey!" Today she was dressed in all red: red shirt, red jeans that were too big for her and cuffed multiple times at the ankles, and scuffed red sneakers. Her hair was pulled on top of her head in a red scrunchy. She'd clearly dressed herself.

Behind them, Aidan banged out of the house and clomped to the top of the steps. "Ella! Best power forward of them all!" They exchanged a high-five secret handshake thing that ended with a sideways hop.

God, the man was adorable. How was a girl supposed to deal with a man who was built like a lumberjack and who also knew how to hop like a bunny?

Then he looked at her, and Tuesday forgot she'd left the bathroom to run away from him. Those eyes. They melted her.

"Hey, check out the bathroom before you leave the site today, okay?"

"The bathroom I just left?"

"If by just you mean thirty minutes ago, yeah."

Surprised, Tuesday glanced at her phone. It *had* been half an hour that she'd been sitting with Felicia. She'd forgotten how good it felt to chat with a girlfriend, how fast the time sped by when she was.

Diana, I miss you so much it hurts.

In two years, the girls would be Ella's age.

In one year, they would have been in her classroom.

Tuesday'd *had* to leave. She cleared her throat. "What's up, Ella? You look like you're on a mission."

Ella nodded firmly. "I am."

"Yeah?"

"Mom's at work, like *always*, but she told me to come talk to you."

Next to Tuesday, Felicia looked at her cell phone and gave a quiet groan. She stood, slipping into her sandals. "Editing snafu. I'll be back."

Tuesday patted the seat of the swing. "Want to sit with me?" She ignored Aidan, still leaning on the porch rail.

"Yeah, okay." Ella wound her way up the porch like a cat, slowly and carefully, but with enough assurance that she didn't look nervous. She sat next to Tuesday and gave the swing a tentative push.

Aidan was smoldering—she felt her cheeks heating. He smiled. The creases at the corners of his eyes were almost as sexy as the ones at his mouth. Tuesday's mother had a saying for people like him. *He's growing into his face.*

God, *she* was growing into his face.

He'd said something that she'd missed. "What?"

"I said, I've done something in the last thirty minutes."

"Hmmm. Why does that make me suspicious?"

He just smiled at her.

Was this what Darling Bay was?

Sitting around outside, neighbors and friends gathering on the porch?

Because not even Minnesota was that friendly, and Minnesotans were *known* for their niceness.

It felt good, this gathering.

It felt kind of...

It felt right.

"Tuesday?" Ella poked her gently in the thigh. "Are you listening?"

"I'm sorry! I'm spacing out today." Spacing out, imagining that this could be her place. Right here. "What did you say?"

Ella's expression was two parts confidence, one part worry. Her mouth smiled, but her eyes stayed wary. "Mom said to come over and ask if you could show me the geometry thing with the angles. She says this afternoon would be perfect because she's got to work, and she's trying not to leave me alone in the house as much. Like, I guess it would be babysitting, but I'm not a baby, so you don't have to worry about that."

Tuesday's first, immediate urge was to say yes. Obviously. This was a girl who needed tutoring, and something in her face said that she needed more. She needed to matter to someone. Tuesday had known so many kids like that in the past.

But her second urge thumped the first with a huge, heavy fist. *I can't.*

She couldn't just say no, not like that. "I want to help you, but oh, this just isn't a good time. You know." She waved a hand behind her. "The remodeling."

Ella's expression shuttered closed. "Oh."

Aidan said, "We can spare you. Go for it."

Panic swept into Tuesday's chest like a storm. "I'm probably not up on your math. Do you have a friend you can—"

Ella shook her head.

Tuesday wanted to take it back, to grab the child and hug her, to fix it all.

But she couldn't. The panic grew higher, and her chest tightened.

Aidan was staring at her.

"I'm sorry. I'm so sorry, but I just can't be..."

"I get it," said Ella, sounding older. "I thought, because you were a teacher, you would—it's fine."

"I can't be responsible for anyone right now." Not even a little bit. For a second, talking to Felicia, she'd thought she was feeling better. But now—it wasn't fair to this girl to let her think otherwise.

Aidan's eyebrows rose.

Tuesday's stomach felt like she'd swallowed glass.

Ella stood, looking older than eleven. "It's really okay."

"I can't tell you how sorry I am."

"It's because of my scar. You can just say it."

"What?" Tuesday was horrified. "Of course not."

She raised a shoulder and dropped it, raising her hand to cover her neck. "I'm used to it, don't worry."

"Honey, I showed you my scar. I'm the last person to care."

"Yeah, well, yours is a good one. It's hidden. It means you can't have babies, so what? Who cares? Mine is on my *face*. I have to live with it every second of the day."

"Ella." Acid burned its way up Tuesday's throat. "You're beautiful."

Without saying another word, Ella ran down the lawn, across to her gate. She kept her left hand clasped against her neck the whole way.

"Oh," gasped Tuesday.

Aidan's voice was quiet. "You said you wanted kids."

She *did* want kids. She wanted them so much that when she'd woken up from surgery and learned that they hadn't been able to put her back together, she'd wanted to die. "I lied." It was a lie in itself.

"Oh, my God."

She doubled down. Why shouldn't she? "Don't you think I get enough of children at school? Don't you think I'm sick of them when I get home?" She wished violently that it was the truth.

"I can see that. Ella looked like you'd stabbed her. But you said—"

Pain was bright behind her eyes. "I had just slept with you. I would have said anything."

"This whole big house—"

"*That's* what this is about," she realized. "It's about the house. The house of your dreams happened to have a woman attached. That was fine, if the woman could breed for you."

"Bullshit." His voice was a dark as his expression.

"Is it? Think about it. You hated me until you realized I wasn't going anywhere. Then you figure out a way to get exactly what you want, a house full of kids, and a teacher to take care of them. Just like Mrs. Brown. Is that who I was supposed to be in this fantasy? The problem is that this is *my* house. If I want to go travel the world and rent it out on Airbnb, I can. I can let it stand empty if I want to. I won't be that perfect little teacher for you." The words felt vicious, sharp. She threw them like darts at a board, and she knew without looking that she was hitting bullseyes.

That was the worst part. That her words were true.

"Tuesday, that's such bullshit that I can't even—"

"You didn't see me for who I was. Who I am." It hurt like the steering wheel had except this wound would probably take longer to heal. "I thought I was falling in love with you."

The slightest smile lit his eyes. "Yeah?"

"Oh, don't worry. I won't, now that I know who you are."

The smile died. "And who's that?"

"A guy so far into doing his own thing that he didn't think to consult the person he chose to say he fell in love with."

Aidan turned so that he leaned on the porch railing. Both hands gripped the wood, his knuckles whitening. She could only see the side of his face. "So you think *I* was lying to you."

Tuesday shook her head. "I think you were lying to yourself."

"About what?"

"About who you thought you were, who you thought you could be."

He turned smoothly, his face a mask. "Darlin', I'm not the one lying about who I am, it turns out."

"I only lied about wanting kids."

"What if everything about you is a lie?"

It felt like she'd run headlong into something hard and tall and heavy. "Stop."

"I think that's it." He nodded and rubbed the bridge of his nose. "You come across as plain. Boring."

Tuesday lifted her jaw. "Awesome, thank you. You're so good at this."

He raised his palm. "Wait. Then you turn on the juice—"

Fury lit her brain, hot and white. "The *juice?*"

"And you dazzle. You're incredible. You're sweet. You're loving."

"We shouldn't—let's not do this."

"Let me finish. You want community. You want to fit in, and everyone falls in love with you."

"Aidan—"

"But you don't fall in love with anything. That's your secret. You keep yourself apart, so that you can be safe. You won't drive because you won't take responsibility for anyone else. You probably don't want to take responsibility for anyone you're on the road with, either."

He was so right it hurt.

Aidan went on. "But it comes down to this: you don't give a good goddamn who you hurt, as long as you keep yourself warm and dry. You know what? I thought I was lonely."

"You think you see me? You think you *know* me?"

He went on as if she hadn't spoken. "But I wasn't. Now I see that. I'm surrounded by people who care about me. That's the opposite of lonely. You, on the other hand—yeah, enjoy the ivory tower you're closing yourself up in."

"Aidan, I never meant to—"

"That's your whole problem. You never meant to. Your intention was to take care of yourself. Congratulations. You've done exactly that. And no more."

Tears burned the backs of her eyelids, and she blinked hard to try to keep them back.

He swung himself down the porch. He turned right and walked up the white rock path that led around the house, to the driveway.

She was left alone.

Like she'd wanted.

Tuesday might as well start getting used to it.

She looped her shoulders back and went inside. The bathroom—she needed to check what he'd meant about the bathroom.

Upstairs, the hardware in the bathroom had been affixed.

Chrome.

Fury coursed through her veins like ice water.

Each and every handle and pull had been put on. The faucet handles were installed.

The chrome looked good, she had to admit. He'd been right (of course he was—this was his job).

But it wasn't the black enamel they'd looked at it in the catalog. It wasn't the black enamel that *she'd* chosen.

That meant that he'd heard her and ordered his choice anyway.

Because he was still thinking about this as his house.

His house, that came with the new addition of female built right in. A broken female, of course. A woman he wouldn't want now that he knew she was faulty. Aidan was the kind of man who built things strong because it was the right thing to do.

She used to be strong. She hadn't been for a long time.

Time for that to change.

She went to find Felicia.

CHAPTER THIRTY-ONE

"She wants out." Felicia dropped her clipboard into a bag at her feet.

Aidan felt a juddering in his chest. It had been two days since he'd fought with Tuesday on the back porch. He hadn't seen her on site, and he hadn't called her.

"What?"

Felicia pinned her scowl on him. "And this is all your fault. She wanted black enamel in that bathroom—you knew that. Why did you put in the chrome?"

Aidan braced an arm against the kitchen sink. "That's not what she's upset about."

"No, you're right." Felicia carefully slipped her iPad into her bag next to the clipboard and then put her hands on her hips. "She's upset at the fact the people she's employing aren't respecting her wishes."

Ow. "Fine. I honestly thought she would like it better. I guess I'll just rip it out."

"You're not hearing me. She wants out. Of the whole thing."

Jake, who'd been quiet till then, stepped forward. "What do we have to do to keep her?"

Aidan's rage was lit with his brother's match. "*Keep* her? I couldn't get out of the contract, neither can she!"

"Actually, she can. It's her money."

"What about the down payment the network is making?"

"She says she has the money to cover it, and that if we don't go along with her, she'll pull all the way out."

"What about the contract?"

"She had a kill clause."

His chest burned. "I said, fine! I'll put in the damned enamel."

"Yeah, you need to do that. Just finish the house. And Aidan?"

Aidan pretended interest in the cabinet. "*This* is what you got for a replacement, Jake? You think this is good wood?"

Jake glared.

"*Aidan.*" Felicia's voice was firm. "Why wouldn't you just do it her way? She won't go on any more dates. She asked that if we move forward, that we broadcast both dates, with you and Jake, and make that be enough."

"So I'm being rejected, too." That felt about right. He'd watched Tuesday shut down Ella, now she was shutting down him, as well. Of course, he'd already been shut out, back when she'd lied to him at the hot spring.

She hadn't trusted him.

It felt like getting cut with a band saw. Then again, why would she trust him? A blue-collar builder like him?

He snapped his fingers at the closest cameraperson, who was drinking a bottled water in the hallway. "Hey. Get this on tape, would you?"

Felicia's eyes widened, but she didn't stop him. Of course not. Drama made for better TV.

When the camera's red light was on, he said, "This is to you, Tuesday. For whenever you see it. I fell in love with you. That was my bad, I know that. If my putting chrome handles in the bathroom was enough to shake you loose? Well, then I'm glad you're cutting me. You should see me when I have opinions about paint colors." He *wasn't* glad, though. He felt gutted, like a flapping cod dying on the old pier. "My stepfather Bill always said I was the one most like my real father. I can see that now. I fell for the wrong woman, just like my father did." He turned and walked away, ignoring Jake's yell from behind him.

Aidan would finish this house for Tuesday, and by God, he'd work the crew faster than they'd ever gone.

Then he'd forget the woman who'd made him feel like he could fly without wings.

CHAPTER THIRTY-TWO

Two weeks and one day later, Tuesday walked from the Cat's Claw to the Callahan house—*her* house. Nerves were dancing in her stomach, and she felt sick. Her skin was clammy and sweat dripped inside her bra even though it was chilly out.

She and caught sight of herself in the big plate glass window of the dance studio. The mirror at the bed and breakfast had said that she looked okay. Tired, yes, but probably all right for one more on-camera shot.

Now, looking at herself on the sidewalk, Tuesday thought she'd never looked worse.

The blue V-necked shirt was limp, too loose at the bust. The dark blue skirt (just the color of Aidan's eyes, damn him) made her look more hippy than she was. She'd worn flats, which had been a mistake because now she just looked short and dumpy. Her glasses flashed in the sun, and her hair was already messed up from the ocean wind.

She would let the hair girl fix her, but no more makeup. She wore the red lipstick that her mother had given her, the one that stuck like glue. That would have to be enough.

The network was making her go through the house on camera now that it was finished. It had been easier to agree than argue with them—they'd caved to all her other demands. They wouldn't make her go on another date. She didn't have to fake working on the house on camera. No diary cams.

No Aidan.

In return, they could still air the episode. All she had to do was a quick walk-through and accept the key from the Ballard Brothers.

She could do it.

If she didn't actually die while filming it.

The house looked quiet from the street. No banging, no hammering. The paint looked wonderful, blue and purple with touches of white—back to the colors that had most likely been original.

A cameraperson popped his head out the front door. "Felicia! She's here!"

"Great!" Felicia tumbled out. Was it possible that she was starting to show already? Tuesday brought her eyes up from Felicia's stomach and smiled.

"Hi."

Felicia's responding smile was thin. "Okay, we'll do this fast and dirty, okay?" She didn't meet Tuesday's eyes. Of course not. Felicia's loyalty lay with her partner's brothers. To the Ballards.

Not to Tuesday. "Okay."

"You've seen the show. I'll walk you up, and you keep your eyes covered. When you're ready, you open, and act surprised, like you're seeing it all for the first time, okay?" Felicia lifted her voice to a yell. "Guys! Everyone out here! Now!"

Felicia herded her down a block. They stood together silently, watching a small white dog attempt to play with a cat across the street. The cat was winning—every time the dog danced close, the cat gave it another swipe.

Tuesday shivered in the blue wool coat which had looked cute earlier, but in the glass window had just looked bulky and out of fashion. "It's cold."

"Mmmm." Felicia made a note on her iPad.

Two cameras arrived, and someone attached a mic pack to her lower back. A hair style was quickly attempted and just as quickly abandoned. The network obviously wanted out as soon as possible, too.

"Ready?"

No.

Tuesday nodded.

The cameras turned on, and so did Felicia. "Tuesday! What an exciting day! Today you're going to see how the house of your dreams turned out. Are you ready?"

Tuesday tried grinning. It felt like a grimace. "So ready!"

"Okay, great! Cover your eyes. No peeking! I'll guide you."

Felicia led her to the house, keeping up a steady stream of positive chatter. Tuesday laughed in all the right places, though her heart felt made of lead and twice as heavy.

"Here we are! Don't peek yet!"

"I'm not!" chirped Tuesday as brightly as she could, ready to cry.

"Three, two, and...one! Open!"

On the porch, all three Ballard brothers stood waving. Liam grinned. Jake smiled.

Aidan, she could see, was trying to smile but failing. He pulled in his lips and shot her a resolute and ironic thumb's up.

Tuesday burst into tears.

"Right?" said Felicia. "The old house looks gorgeous, doesn't she? Wait till you see what we've done inside!"

The men parted to let her and the cameras inside.

It only took a few minutes. Tuesday cried and hiccupped her way through her house.

The furnishings were perfect and new.

There were books in the shelves, and they weren't hers. The new dining table filled the space beautifully, the wood polished to a high red gloss.

Everything felt empty. Soulless.

The bedroom was prettily done up with all white furnishings. They'd given her a skylight and bigger windows, so she could see the marina from the second floor.

The bathroom tile was done. The clawfoot tub was in.

The fixtures were black enamel.

And they looked awful. The chrome really had been better.

She smiled through her tears and said, "I just can't believe it. Any of it." At least everything she said was true.

She couldn't believe she'd lost him.

She couldn't believe she'd hurt Ella.

She couldn't believe she'd gotten it all so spectacularly wrong.

In the kitchen, they poured champagne into glasses, even though it wasn't even eleven in the morning.

"Where would you like to drink your toast to your new home, Tuesday?" Felicia was so sparkly—she was *good* at her job.

"How about—" Tuesday hiccupped again "the porch?" Outside, she needed to be out, not so close to Aidan that she could smell the pine of his body as she could in the kitchen.

Outside, Tuesday's eye was drawn to the hang gliders down at the water.

She had soared like that.

Once.

God, she needed this to end so she could christen her new bed with two or three years' worth of tears. She raised her glass. "To home!"

"To home." Glasses clinked.

Tuesday sucked back half the glass, hiccupping more violently when she stopped.

Felicia nodded at her.

Right. She had lines to deliver. *Diana, I can't do this. I'm not strong enough.*

She took a deep breath. "I had a great time... Um." She shook her head.

Gene, the cameraman, looked over the lens.

"That's okay," said Felicia. "Just start over."

She'd go fast, hitting the lines they'd told her to hit. "I had a great time dating Jake and Aidan Ballard, but they're both still on the market."

"Any regrets about putting Jake in the hospital?" Felicia made it sound like it had been her plan.

"Sorry about that, Jake."

He smiled at her and it almost looked genuine. "No problem. My head is hard as a rock."

"And you're not picking Aidan, either?" pressed Felicia.

Her heart felt wrung dry. "Well, I knew that moment that he bashed in the wrong wall that maybe he wasn't the one for me." Oh, God. Tuesday had meant it to come out light. A little joke. A reference to something funny that had happened that would make them all laugh.

But Aidan's face grew darker. Then it went red.

She'd *embarrassed* him.

Even Jake looked disappointed in her.

"I mean, I'm just joking. I'm sorry. I didn't mean that."

Felicia sighed. "Can you just deliver the last line, please?"

Shit, shit, shit. "Yes. Of course." She tried to put lightness into her voice and face, but she could still feel the wetness of her tears on her cheeks. "But this house is off the market! And it's all mine."

Aidan's eyes, when she said the last three words, were so dark and blank that she shivered.

"Are we done?" he said.

Felicia barely looked up. "Yeah. Thanks."

Aidan ripped of his mic, spun on his boot heel, and leaped off the porch. He was around the house and gone before Tuesday could even think of another word to say to him.

Her heart was ragged, shredded.

The key Liam had handed her sat in her palm. It felt heavier than any key she'd ever touched.

Weakly, she slid it into her pocket and held her breath. Soon, she'd be alone.

Then she could really cry.

CHAPTER THIRTY-THREE

Aidan left.

He shouldn't leave the site, he knew that. There were probably finishing touches he could help with. Make sure the crew picked everything up. Check the lock on the basement.

But he got in his truck anyway, brought it to life and roared down the driveway toward town.

Away from her.

He drove in a circle for a while, waiting. He knew Liam needed to get back to the office—he'd give him half an hour and then go accost him.

How had Aidan's life spiraled like this?

He'd been getting *paid* to date the woman of his dreams.

He'd been falling in love.

No, goddamn it. He *was* in love. *With an infertile liar.* Shit. He wished he weren't.

Jesus, he'd imagined Tuesday in a wedding dress. Wasn't that exactly what a red-blooded American male *wasn't* supposed to think about? But the image had made his mouth dry. He'd wanted to see her walking down an aisle toward him, her eyes lit with unabashed joy.

He was such an idiot.

He pulled up at the marina and watched three fishing trawlers putt in. He considered buying a six-pack and drinking them all in his truck. Instead, he started the engine and burned out of the parking lot. Three more turns, one impulsive and kind of stupid dodge around a slow-ass SUV, and he pulled up in front of the office.

In his mind's eye, he touched his other fantasies to see if they hurt the same way the wedding dress dream did.

He'd imagined sitting on a wide, low couch with her. Out the back windows, the oak boughs danced. Tuesday held a white plastic stick with pink lines on the end. She smiled at him with tears in her eyes, tears that matched his.

Fuck, Ballard. He wasn't an idiot. No, he'd blown right past that and into fucking moron-of-the-century territory.

He stormed up the steps of the Victorian. "Liam! Are you here yet?" His voice came out in a shout. He hadn't meant it to.

Liam looked up from his desk in surprise. He was wearing a black T-shirt instead of the button down he'd had on at the Callahan house. "Why are you roaring like a monster?"

"I want to sell my condo."

Liam carefully put down his pencil. He steepled his fingers. "Why don't you sit down and we can talk about it?"

Did his brother think he was stupid? "That's your customer voice."

"Is it?"

Fine, Liam could play dumb all he wanted, but Aidan knew the tone of voice his brother got when he was mollifying a problem client.

Which he was *totally* willing to become, if that would make the process go faster. "Selling." He jabbed his finger onto the desktop. "The condo. Draw up the paperwork."

"It's not like there's a Sell-Me-Now form that I submit electronically to the state. Sit. Tell me what the hell's up your ass."

Aidan could no more sit than he could do a headstand. "I want to buy a house."

Liam sighed. "You can't buy Tuesday's house."

"Not her house."

"Really? What house, then?"

"Any house. Piece of shit hovel, I don't give a fuck."

"Well, there are plenty of those on the market." Liam shook his head. "But I need more. What's going on?"

"I can't have the house I wanted." Or the woman. "So I'll just buy a different one."

"You *might* be moving too fast."

"You ain't seen fast yet. How soon can I sell the condo?"

"Come on. Even if we had a buyer right now, which we don't, it would take a month. And your place isn't even ready to be put on the market, am I right?"

"It's ready."

"Did you even ever finish painting?"

Aidan scowled.

"Or finishing those cabinets?"

"You think I don't do enough sanding at work? It's the last thing I want to do when I get home."

"Fine. What I'm saying is it'll take a while." Liam punched his keyboard. "But while I'm pulling some comps, you tell me what's going on. This is about Tuesday, right?"

Aidan lowered his eyebrows so much he could almost see them. "No."

Liam laughed.

The ass-hat *laughed.* "I hate you."

Liam shrugged. "Yeah, I'm not too worried about that. I gotta say, seems like she's gotten under your skin."

"Like scabies."

Liam winced. "Or like love."

"Fuck love."

"Sore spot?"

Aidan would show Liam sore. "Shut *up.*"

"Make me," said Liam lightly. "Okay, we're looking at about two-fifty for condos that size on the east side of town. Do you think—" He broke off, bouncing a pencil between his fingers.

"What?"

"I just have to say that I like what you're doing."

Good, at least one of them knew what Aidan was doing. "And what's that?"

"Admitting that you can't control the future. Taking a step that isn't planned."

"Excuse me?"

"I'm just saying." Liam smiled. "You've been so closed up for a long time. Unwilling to make any sudden moves."

"*Me?*" He'd made a sudden move, all right. He'd fallen in love with the wrong woman.

"The only thing you've ever committed to is this business and that tiny condo you bought ten years ago. No room for anyone to get close to you. If you kept a girlfriend for more than a month, you'd have to give her at least a drawer in your place, but you always eject before that."

"That's not true."

"Dude. You know it is. Jake and I talk about it all the time."

"You talk about this with Jake?"

"He's worried about you. So am I. We thought Tuesday would be good for you, and I have to say, I still think she is. Even if it's not in the way I thought she would be."

Aidan dropped into the chair, finally. "How was that?"

"I thought you two would fall in love, get married, and fill that house with kids. Your dream."

He'd never actually said that was his dream. Not in so many words. "How did you know that?"

"I remember that crush you had on Mrs. Brown. You've always been hot for teacher, right?"

Aidan snorted. "God."

"You were so funny. You'd go there for dinner, and then for the next week, nothing was good enough for you. They used a different brand of ketchup—"

"Yeah, not generic."

"And you suddenly couldn't use ours. Remember how Bill would tease you about how much it sucked, you having to live in the wrong house?"

Aidan had forgotten that, but as soon as Liam said it, it all came flooding back. Bill had loved them so much, but he'd always felt bad that he hadn't had much money. He remembered driving by Mrs. Brown's house in Bill's old truck. *You wish you could live in a nice house like that one, kiddo?*

Nah.

You don't have to lie about it. It's not a bad thing to want a little more than you have.

"What I don't get," said Liam, "is why you have to do this right now. Why not just wait? We'll get the crew in, do a quick remodel, and sell it for a third more."

"If I sell it fast, with my savings I'll have enough cash to buy a small house outright."

"That's never mattered to you before."

"My house is gone."

Liam said, "Yeah, well, Jake and I have been hoping you would end up in that house anyway. Sideways, like."

He'd hoped that, too. "Never going to happen. And if I spend all my money on a different place, I'll have to fall in love with that instead."

"Does it work like that?"

Aidan pressed his palms together. They were slick with sweat. "It has to."

"If I couldn't be with Felicia, I'd be alone. I wouldn't try to replace her to distract myself."

"That not what I'm doing."

Liam just arched an eyebrow.

Aidan spent twenty long, pleasant seconds hating his brother with every fiber of his being. Then he said, "Will you just sell my fucking place for me?" His voice cracked, and suddenly, he wanted to cry.

Or hit something.

His brother was pretty handy.

As if he felt it, Liam held up his hands in surrender. "Fine. Hey, I saw the dailies for your diary cam. Why did you say that? About Bill? And you being like Dad, choosing the wrong woman?"

"Because it was true. I'm exactly like Dad."

"Where did you get that idea?"

Aidan stared at his brother. "He was talking to *you* when he said it."

"I remember him saying that—"

"That I was the biggest chip off the old block. That I was going to be just like him, and end up in jail or worse."

Liam shook his head, as if to clear it. "I vaguely remember that, but I remember what he said next better."

Aidan had run away, that was true. He hadn't heard whatever Bill had said next. "So? What was that?"

"He said that he was looking forward to watching you grow out of it. That you were going to be the kind of man he'd have coffee with. He said you'd be the one who really made it. And you have."

"Come on." It was a weak protestation. The inside of Aidan's brain felt scoured.

"I remember it exactly. He said I was never going to be the tool guy of the bunch, but that my math skills would help us. And he said you'd be the foreman of our crew someday, and that you'd be good at it. He said you'd be on city council."

Aidan was. He was the most junior council member, but he loved going to the meetings. Other people said they were boring. He thought they had a certain beauty. An order.

"He said you'd the be the first of us to own your own place."

Aidan had bought his condo when he was only twenty-four, years before the three of them bought the Ballard office.

"And he said you'd be the last of us to go to jail because you were the one most scared of being like Dad. He said you'd be the one to soar."

Oh, God.

Liam was still staring at him. "Did you *really* think Bill didn't believe in you?"

"I've thought it since I heard him that night."

"And you've been trying to prove him wrong."

Aidan gave one short nod.

"When all along, Bill was right, and you've turned into exactly the man he thought you would be."

Aidan bit the inside of his cheek so hard he tasted blood. "Dude."

"You've been wrong a long time, then."

Aidan nodded. "Shit." It felt like the word held his soul.

"And now you've lost her, too."

"Because I'm too stupid to live."

"Then do something really smart."

"For once."

"No, you idiot. Like usual."

Liam hugged him then, and Aidan hugged back. He thought about saying *I love you,* but then Liam would take him to the hospital, so he just said, "You smell like dryer sheets."

"Thanks. Back at you."

CHAPTER THIRTY-FOUR

On her new bed for the first time, Tuesday curled up on top of the white bedspread. The whole room smelled like paint, and she was sure she'd forever associate the scent with heartbreak.

Aidan had fallen in love with her.

But the real problem was that she'd fallen back.

And then she'd screwed everything up by not being honest with him—the *one* thing he said he needed.

She'd been alone at home in Minnesota. She'd been content in her singleness. After the accident, her hospital social worker had told her it might take her a long time to want to date again. *You'll get used to the scar, but it might be hard to show it to anyone intimately for a while.* The scar? That was the least of her problems, really. Take a long time to date? It would be forever. She was damaged goods.

Her mother had told her that the right person wouldn't mind the scarring.

Tuesday hadn't told her that wasn't the problem.

She was too scarred inside. No one needed to know that but her. How could she love another person, knowing that a moment of indecision, a second of not paying attention could hurt or kill the person she loved? Her parents thought her refusal to drive was something she'd eventually get over, and she'd let them think that. She agreed with them when they brought it up. Sure, she'd get another car someday, she told them. When the settlement came through, they'd thought she should go buy a nice midsize sedan with some of the money immediately. *Get back up on that horse,* her father said. *You're a good driver,* her mother said. *You don't have to have a passenger for a long time. Years, if that's what it takes.*

It wasn't about the passengers, that was what she'd never told anyone, not even her post-accident therapist. It was about her being in charge of a huge, heavy piece of machinery that she wasn't sure she could always control. What if she had a stroke at the wheel? There was no history in her family—no reason to think she would. But if she did, her car would keep moving, and might hurt someone. It was better not to drive.

Public transportation was nice.

She would keep people from being in danger by not driving, ever again.

She'd never really stopped to think about the danger inherent in being near someone else's heart.

It sure felt like hers was going to stop. How was a heart supposed to keep beating when it hurt to breathe? She remembered coming out of anesthesia, right before they told her they hadn't been able to put her back together. She'd thought the pain was unbearable then, that no one could live through it. She'd whispered it to the nurse, unable to make her voice louder. *I hurt.* They'd upped her painkillers, and told her she couldn't have children, and while the physical pain finally retreated like an angry animal, there was no painkiller strong enough to touch the real pain. *I am unfit.*

She was unsafe for others. She wasn't even a real woman anymore.

The scent of paint was overwhelming. She swore when the walls peeled in the distant future, she'd let them.

Tuesday stood and threw open the French doors. The fug of paint fumes couldn't reach the balcony, thank God. Maybe she'd sleep out here tonight. How cold did it get at night? Would she freeze to death?

Was that a completely terrible proposition?

She'd been holding her cell phone loosely in her hand, unable to decide what to do with it. Should she email her parents?

What she desperately wanted more than anything was to call Diana. To hear her raspy voice, to tell her about Aidan and how stupid she was to fall for a man who wanted to use her to get the house of his dreams. She wanted Diana to tease her, to laugh at her.

Tuesday broke everything.

Absolutely every single little thing.

Her phone buzzed in her hand.

Mom and Dad.

Tuesday shouldn't answer. She should let it roll to voice mail. There was no way she could talk to her mother without crying, and then she'd know—but at the last moment, just before it stopped ringing, she pushed the green button. "Mom?"

"Hiya, you."

The words tumbled out. "I hurt a kid."

An indrawn breath was all she heard. "What do you mean?"

"Not physically." That she had to clarify that made the muscles in her jaw ache. "This girl who lives next door kind of attached herself to me. Fast."

"As kids do."

"She asked for some school help, and I said no."

Her mother laughed. "Is that all you did? Honey."

"You should have seen her face."

"She'll get over it."

"We bonded over our scars."

"Oh..."

"And her mom's never home."

"Honey, you can't take on the whole weight of the world."

Was her mother kidding? Tuesday wasn't taking on anything at all. That was the problem. She was hiding. She'd hurt the first kid who felt comfortable talking to her. "She looked like I'd punched her."

"So go apologize."

"No, way. I'm just going to stay away."

"Because that's what you do now?" Her mother's voice was unexpectedly sharp.

"Pardon?" It felt like a physical blow. It wasn't like Tuesday didn't *know* it. She just didn't think her mother would say it.

"You've turned into someone who runs away."

"Mom—"

"And that's a strategy. Your father and I agree it's fine for now. But if you're going to keep it up then you have to keep your distance from everyone, even the people there, or you'll end up hurting them, too."

"Mom! How long have you thought this?"

A harsh sigh echoed down the phone. "A long time. But you've been acting so damn *fragile.*"

Tuesday could only blink. She had been fragile. That was why she'd acted that way.

"Honey, you've always been so strong. That's what you seem to have forgotten how to be. Remember Thomasina's funeral?"

Thomasina Welks, one of her favorite students, had died of leukemia the year after she'd been in Tuesday's class. Tuesday had planned most of her funeral, since her single mother couldn't get out of bed and she had no other relatives close by. It had been horrible and awful and Tuesday had been honored to do it. To be the strong one. "Yeah."

There was a clatter and then a whine, as if her mother had just put her on speakerphone. Her voice was hollow when she next spoke. "That's how you always were. Ready to bolster anyone. What about Diana?"

"What about her?"

"Have you called her?"

"She doesn't want to hear from me."

Her mother whispered, "*Idiot.*"

"Mom!"

"You didn't support her."

That's not fair.

"Honey, you have to find that core strength inside you again."

"What if it's gone forever?"

"Then you *pretend.*"

"What?"

"It's what the rest of us do every day. We just pretend, and then it becomes real. What are you going to do with that young man of yours?"

Right. Her mother didn't know. "I broke it off with him."

Another long sigh. "Of course you did. You said he was the one."

He was. "He deserved better, Mom."

"Like what?"

"Like a woman who could give him children, for example."

"*Give me the phone, Margo.*"

Tuesday heard a scuffle. Her mother said, "It's on speakerphone, Ron, just talk to her."

Her father bellowed, "*Just trust the man to love you!*"

Salt stung her nose. "Daddy—"

"For the love of God, Tuesday! Give him the damn choice whether he wants to stick around!"

Another clatter. "Figure out how to be strong again. You can do it."

Ten minutes after the call ended, Tuesday still sat in frozen silence. She ached to the center of her perma-chilled bones.

She had gotten everything so very wrong.

A bit of motion down below caught her eye. The gate to the hot spring.

Ella was just disappearing through it.

Tuesday didn't have the bravery.

Not today.

Then she heard her mother's voice in her head. *So go apologize.*

Maybe it was a place to start.

Maybe.

CHAPTER THIRTY-FIVE

Tuesday pushed open the gate.

Ella sat on a low, flat, moss-covered rock, her legs in the water up to her knees. She had a book in her hands, and was looking down at it. She didn't move when the gate creaked.

But she was listening.

If Tuesday knew anything, it was when a child was pretending to not be paying attention.

"What are you reading?"

Casually, Ella turned her head. "Oh, nothing." She closed the book and turned it upside down on her lap, but Tuesday knew the spine at one glance. She'd know it anywhere.

"The Secret Garden, huh? My favorite. I thought this place was like her garden when I first saw it."

Ella didn't answer.

"Did you think of it, too? This place?"

A short nod.

"Can I sit here?" Tuesday pointed at a rock just a few feet away from Ella's.

A quick shrug.

"Thanks." Tuesday put her feet into the water and sighed. "It's heaven."

"The last people to live in your house never let me in here."

"They didn't?"

"That was a couple of years ago. I think they thought I would drown."

"But you're older now."

"And there's the whole hot water thing." Purposefully, Ella touched the scar on her neck.

"Yeah. I get it. Well, you're welcome here."

Ella shrugged.

"I have something to say to you," said Tuesday.

The girl sighed. "Do you have to?"

She sounded like a teenager suddenly. Tuesday realized with a thud that she wanted to be near this girl while she was growing up. She wanted to see the angst, the heartache, the pain, and then the beautiful growth. "I'm so sorry."

Ella kept her eyes forward, watching the steam rise from the center.

"I made you feel like I was rejecting you."

"You did reject me."

"But it really was me."

"It's okay. It's fine." Ella's words painfully echoed Diana's.

"I've heard that before, and it's usually said when something isn't fine. I have to tell you a secret. I didn't tell you before because I was trying to protect myself." Aidan's words echoed in her head. *You don't give a good goddamn who you hurt, as long as you keep yourself warm and dry.* "But I'm learning we can't protect ourselves from everything. It's the reason I came to Darling Bay."

This, at least, got the girl's attention. "Why did you come here?"

"Because I was in a car crash, the one I told you about. Where I got my scar. I had my best friend's kids in the car. Twin girls. They both got hurt. Now they're not twins anymore."

Ella looked startled but then scowled. "Yeah, they are."

"No. One's in a wheelchair, and the other has a scarred face. All because I wasn't paying attention to my responsibilities."

"That's so stupid."

It was a jolt. "What?"

"I mean, sure you feel bad, but it's not like you're God or something. They're still twins."

"But—"

"I get it. They look different. But I bet *they* still feel like twins. I know that. I've always wanted one. I wouldn't care if she looked different from me, I'd just care that we were together."

Tuesday shivered again even though the heat of the water on her legs was making her sweat. "Are you a little bit mad, though?"

"At you?"

"No. At the person who put the water on the stove, the pan that you pulled down." Ella would say yes. It would prove Tuesday's point.

"Of course not." Ella rolled her eyes. "It was an *accident.*"

She made it sound so simple.

So simple.

"I'm sorry."

"It's okay," Ella said again.

"Really, I saw your face when I said I wouldn't help, and it broke my heart."

A smile finally broke over Ella's face, and it was like the sun coming out. "Fine. My mom always says you have to either accept an apology or not. So I accept it."

Relief tasted like honey in Tuesday's mouth. "My mom says the same thing."

"Moms." Ella put her hands on the rock behind her and leaned back, looking up at the sky that was just beginning to clear.

"Moms," agreed Tuesday, doing the same.

"So you're staying?"

"I think so." If she could keep her broken heart from bleeding all over the place when she passed Aidan on the street, in the café, in the bar.

"I'm glad."

"Why?"

"Because I liked you from the very start."

"Ditto, Ella." Tuesday felt the tiniest sprig of hope uncurl in her heart, green and strong. "Ditto."

CHAPTER THIRTY-SIX

Aidan had a mission. Finally.

He sat on the brown leather couch in the small living room of his small condo, his laptop balanced on his knees. The small clock on the mantel chimed the half hour. The falcon painted on the clock's face raised its wings to either side of its glass face.

Aidan had always thought Bill had given the clock to him because Aidan was late too often. And maybe that was partially true.

But maybe it was also because Bill knew he'd always loved tracing the falcon on the clock with his finger.

Maybe it was because Bill thought he would someday soar like the bird.

Aidan felt the tattoo under his shirt grow warm as he looked around the living room with new eyes. *I hate this place.*

He'd been angry when he'd asked Liam to list the condo, but it had been the right thing to do. He'd buy a different house and start over.

Maybe he'd bring nothing with him but that clock.

Start fresh.

He fired up Facebook. He had a hundred and twenty-three notifications waiting for him, but considering that he hadn't logged on in at least six months, that didn't seem too bad.

Two or three clicks got him to Tuesday's Facebook page, which was unlocked, lucky for him. There was no Diana listed under her friends (who had unfriended whom?) but there was a Margo Willis, who looked like an older version of Tuesday. Funny, she should have been plain—with her mousy gray hair, wire-rimmed glasses, and medium brown eyes—but there was a twinkle in her eye that Aidan recognized. A particular sparkle that lit up the older woman.

God, this had to work. This much hope had never traveled through his fingers. From Margo's page, he found a Diana Majors. Was that her, maybe?

Yes, it had to be. Diana's page was locked down, but her profile picture showed a pretty dark-haired woman with two girls flanking her. One girl had a shiny pink scar running from the side of her nose to under her jaw.

As Aidan hit the Friend request button, his heart pounded like he'd just shifted a pallet of roof tiles.

With any luck, she was online.

But on second thought, what woman these days accepted the friending by a man across the country, a man she didn't know or have connection to—

There it was.

Diana Majors had confirmed his friendship.

Holy shit.

Was this like putting in the chrome in the bathroom? Was he overstepping Tuesday's wishes again? How was he supposed to know if he was screwing all of this up?

Aidan put his fingers on the keyboard and closed his eyes. Feeling slightly stupid, he waited to see what he felt.

It felt right. The chrome had been a push.

This was different—he didn't have Tuesday, but maybe he could help make her life better anyway.

He wasn't a good typist—more of a hunt-and-pecker—but he was fast.

Dear Ms. Majors,

I have come to know Tuesday Willis.

God, that sounded weird.

Tuesday Willis is a friend of mine.

If Diana and Tuesday weren't friends anymore, that might sound like a weird type of bragging.

I've fallen in love with Tuesday Willis.

In for a penny, right?

I really don't know how you two left it between you, and it's none of my business, I know that. But I bet this is what happened: Tuesday panicked and ran. That's what I would have done if I were in her shoes. My brother is going to be a father, and suddenly, the one thing I don't want to do is hold that baby because I'll be so afraid of dropping it.

But I will. Because that's what family does.

When she talks about you, it sounds like she's talking about family.

I can't fix anything between the two of you, and it's more than possible you don't want it to be fixed. If that's so, please delete this message, no hard feelings.

But first, I want to tell you this: She's been writing you an email for months. She says she writes it late at night and early the morning. She says she tells you everything.

You should ask her to send it to you.

I blew it. I stepped over her wishes, and I assumed about a thing I should never have assumed. You want the truth? I thought it was a sign when the woman of my dreams moved into the house I've always wanted.

I assumed too much.

But you have the history with her.

She loves me.

He looked at the sentence for a long moment, and then erased the last word. His lungs hurt from holding his breath.

She loves you.

He clicked send.

The falcon clock chimed the next quarter hour. That had only taken fifteen minutes.

Now what the hell was he supposed to do with the rest of his life?

CHAPTER THIRTY-SEVEN

Sitting at the kitchen island, Tuesday finished digitally signing the employment application. It was a formality—the local school district was short on fifth and sixth grade teachers and the superintendent had told her she was in.

Good. That was good.

That's what she kept telling herself.

Tuesday clicked send, and the application on its way to the district office. Out the window, she saw the mailman walk by. She raised her hand in case he could see her inside the house.

He waved back cheerfully. Damn, she'd forgotten his name again. She *had* to get that right soon.

Tuesday would have a job and a home in Darling Bay. Exactly what she'd wanted. Her parents were coming to visit the next week, and they were thinking about buying a small place in the area. She'd had a friend-date coffee with Felicia, and Tuesday had been the one to start the baby-is-coming conversation. By choice. She'd honestly wanted to know.

It didn't hurt. Not like she'd thought it would.

Maybe losing the man she loved made losing imaginary babies she could never have a little easier.

Her cell jangled with a text.

Send me the email.

The skin of Tuesday's face tingled, as if she'd been slapped. How did Diana know? How *could* she—

Aidan.

He was the only one she'd told about the ongoing drafted email. He had *told* her? How? Tuesday went cold at her very core.

The text sat on the screen, making the phone feel heavier.

Dread.

And hope.

In equal parts.

Diana knew? And she wanted the email?

Well, hell. She could have it, then.

Tuesday pulled up the drafted email as she did every day. Her trigger finger hovered over the send button. She should at least reread it a few times.

No, goddamn it, she didn't *need* to read it—she knew it by heart. She knew every *I'm sorry* and *I love you* and *I'm so so so sorry*. She knew every *I have to tell you that* and *I'm worried that.*

God, she was being cautious again. Always so careful, especially when it came to anything about emotion.

Her finger landed on the computer keyboard with a heavy thud. She hit send.

Then she covered her mouth. "Oh, *shit*." She shouldn't have done that without reading it.

The whole thing was a love letter.

An apology.

An entreaty.

And she'd just sent it.

Tuesday stared at her phone in abject terror. The kitchen, normally her favorite place in the house, seemed suddenly too small. The walls closed around her, and for a second she longed for Aidan's sledgehammer.

Seven and a half minutes later, her phone rang.

Tuesday stared at Diana's face on the screen of her phone—she hadn't seen that photo in so long she forgot it flashed when Diana called.

It rang again.

It took every ounce of bravery she'd ever felt, all piled together, to answer. "Hello?"

"You *left* me."

Tuesday choked on the lump that rendered her temporarily unable to speak. "Diana—"

"You left us."

"I'm sorry."

"You're *not* sorry. That's the thing. You've gone to this new town, and you love it, and you have the best house, with a natural hot spring, and you're having hot sex with that guy Aidan—"

She'd read the email.

Oh, God.

"And it seems like you love it there, and this whole email made me miss you so much I honestly want to punch you in the nose."

Tuesday gasped a laugh. Once, at a movie theater, Diana *had* punched Tuesday in the nose while putting on her coat. "You're good at that."

"No, like *really* punch you. Hard."

"I would deserve it." That and so much more. *She'd hurt Diana's children.*

"Not for the accident, you complete and total idiot. For leaving me behind without even saying goodbye."

"I couldn't."

"You could have. And you should have."

"I know."

"Then why didn't you?"

Tuesday clenched her free hand into a fist so hard her fingers ached. "You know why."

"Because I forgave you?"

"No."

"Because you didn't believe I forgave you."

"Yes." That was it. That was the truth. Now it was out there.

"Yeah, well, who makes *you* the person who gets to decide what my words mean? You don't get to do that. I get to decide how I feel, and you deciding I feel differently means that you're not listening, that you're not trusting me."

"You're right."

"And by the way—wait. What?" There was a clatter on the end of the line, as if Diana had dropped something.

"You're totally right. I should have believed you."

Diana's voice was almost a whisper. "What *happened* to you out there?"

"I...I fell in love."

"You poor thing."

"You should know."

"I do."

"How's Nicholas?"

"Handsome as ever. And twice as annoying." The fondness in Diana's voice warmed Tuesday to her bones.

"How are the girls?"

Diana's tone softened. "They're good. They're really just fine, Tuesday. They miss you."

"I'm so sorry, Diana."

"For what, exactly? I just want to hear it."

"For everything."

An impatient huff. "You can do better than that."

It was true, she could. Tuesday kept her eyes fixed on the white mailbox that was painted with her house's numbers. "I'm sorry I didn't listen to you. That I didn't believe you forgave me."

"The worst thing you ever did was leave without saying goodbye."

"Diana—"

"But if you bring that man back with you the next time you come home, I might consider forgiving you for that, too."

Had she not read the whole email? Didn't she know that Tuesday had blown it? She'd hurt everyone that mattered. Well, Diana would be able to watch the episode soon enough—the whole world would see Tuesday pick a stupid house over the love of her life. "No, he's gone."

"Why'd he go to all that trouble to get you back on the phone with your best friend?"

The sudden burst of radiant hope was too blinding—Tuesday had to close her eyes. "I don't know. Oh, God. What do I do?"

"You go talk to him."

"I think I hurt him too much."

"Just go ask him. Talk to him. And Tuesday?"

"Yeah?"

"Believe what the man says. People say things for a reason, and you have to trust them. You don't *earn* love. You have it or you don't."

"And what if I don't?"

"Just go talk to him."

"Diana?"

"Yeah?"

Tuesday's heart beat so hard she could feel her pulse fluttering in her neck. "I missed you so much."

CHAPTER THIRTY-EIGHT

Tuesday had been to the Ballard Brothers' office three or four times, usually with Felicia, always to sign something. The old house was fitted with an office in the front, and living space in the back—it was attractive if a little rough around the edges.

Liam stood up from his desk. He looked surprised to see her, but not displeased. "If you're here to talk to him, you couldn't have come at a better time. I've told him to turn down the music three times. Maybe he'll listen to you."

The back workshop was to the side of the property, down a short driveway. "He's in there. It looks like a garage but it hasn't held a car in fifty years." The banging that was thundering out the building competed with the decibel level of the pulsing rock music. "Get him to shut that down, would you?"

Liam turned and went back to the main house.

Tuesday wanted to follow him. Her body felt boneless, as if she were floating toward the workshop. But she heard her shoes scuff the gravel, and overhead, an enormous bird landed in a sycamore, the branch giving an ominous crack. She looked up.

A falcon. A smallish one, red tailed and sleek-feathered, it tilted its head to look at her.

It was a sign.

The problem was Tuesday had no idea what the sign meant. Did it mean she was doing the right thing?

Or was it warning her to run?

She turned in place twice.

She would knock on the shed's door.

No, she would leave.

One more pivot.

"Are you doing some kind of dance out here?"

Tuesday froze, mid spin. "Um."

"Because it's weird."

She turned to face him. God, he was glorious. He wore a tight T-shirt which had once been white and was now streaked with grease and ripped at the hem. Old jeans. Black scuffed boots. Two days' worth of stubble, and a look in his eyes like he'd just lost a boxing match. He held a wrench in his hand.

Tuesday struggled to breathe.

"Yeah?"

She pointed upward. "Is that a falcon?"

Aidan's head went back. "Oh, damn."

"It is, right?" She focused on his Adam's apple in an effort to avoid staring at the rest of his body.

"Yeah."

"Is that a sign?"

He shrugged. "If you say it is."

"Aidan—"

He sighed. "If you've got something to say, why don't you just get on with it so I can get back to work."

This was too hard.

She couldn't do it.

Diana's voice rang clear in her head: *Just tell him.*

"I need a widow's walk built. I was wondering if you did that kind of work."

He rubbed his eyes with one hand. "What?"

"Widow's walk. It's this raised level of a house—"

"Obviously, I know what it is. But what are you talking about? You're leaving town."

"I'm what?"

"You said you were." He shoved the wrench into his back pocket.

"I didn't."

"You said you were going to put the house on Airbnb."

"Oh, God. I didn't mean it. I just said I could, if I wanted to. I was trying to prove a point."

"Do you *ever* take words seriously? Do they matter to you at all?"

Tuesday pressed her heels together in an effort to stand still. Instead, she just felt wobbly. "I do. I swear I do."

"Why, then? Why the widow's walk?"

Tuesday had thought it had taken courage to answer Diana's call. That courage was nothing compared to what she needed to dredge from the bottom of her soul now.

She took a deep breath. "Because I want to stand watch up there. I want to wait for the man I love to come home."

"Oh." He shoved his hands into his front pockets. "You dating a sailor now?"

She shook her head. "He flies."

Aidan's dark blue eyes heated, and though he didn't move a muscle, Tuesday could feel something shift between them. "He does, huh."

"And I worry."

"About what?"

"Statistics. That one in a thousand fatality rate."

"What right do you have to worry about him?" Aidan stuck out his jaw, but his eyes said everything else that she needed to hear.

"I'm in love with him."

"What if he doesn't love you back?"

She echoed his words, the one he'd said weeks ago, in the bathroom of her new house. "Then I'm doomed. Already gone. I'll just enjoy it as much as possible."

He took one step toward her as if he were been dragged. As if he couldn't help it. "You lied to me."

"I did." Tuesday felt sweat start on her hairline. "And I'm very sorry. That was wrong, and I wish I hadn't. I just didn't want you to see me as broken, even though that's exactly what I am."

Aidan took one more step toward her. "You think I care?"

"You said you wanted your kids to have their mother's mouth."

He shook his head. "I don't give a crap. I just happened to be looking at your mouth when I said that. You know the man who raised me, who made me into the man I am—we had nothing in common biologically. But he was my real father, and my whole life is built around making that man proud."

Tuesday's fingers started shaking. "Oh."

"I thought you were like a robin."

Her heart stuttered. "I can see that comparison."

"But you're more like the falcon." He gestured upward, but didn't lift his eyes from her face. "Because you can see a long, long way."

"I could see farther if I had a widow's walk. And someone to build it for me."

One more step closer. "You'll have to call it something else. I don't like thinking of you as a widow."

Tuesday held her breath for a long moment, so long that bright sparks skittered at the edge of her vision. "What would I be instead?"

He closed the last step between them. "Mine."

"Build it strong, so it doesn't fall off this time." She put her hand on his chest. His heart thundered against her fingertips.

"That's what I do best."

She smiled at him. "No, it's not."

With a groan, he pulled her against him. "Jesus, woman."

"I love you." It was so sweet on her tongue. She wanted to say it until she ran out of air, out of life itself. "I love you."

His kiss was all the answer she needed, but a moment later he pulled away, his voice taut with need. "I never wanted your damn house, you know."

"You didn't?"

"I thought I was looking for a home, but I was looking for you."

"Well, fancy that." Tuesday said. "I was looking for you, too."

Behind them, the falcon fell from its perch on the sycamore bough. It caught itself, much like a hang glider does after running off a cliff. The falcon soared upward, kept aloft by a thermal caused by the sudden heat of a kiss that promised forever and maybe a little longer.

EPILOGUE

Aidan was tired. It had been an extra long day—from the moment he'd rolled out of bed, untangling himself from Tuesday's warm, soft limbs, he'd been on the run. He'd had to oversee the insulation work at the Mantel's house, then he had to run to the network's job site (Jake now had to date every single woman who bought a house for *On the Market,* and he was loving his new role) where they'd found an extreme and unreported termite infestation.

Then, like he did every day, he went to the house he'd bought with the money he'd made from selling the condo.

The sign had just gone up, dark green with white lettering. *Ballard Youth.*

It made his chest feel full, just to look at it. Bill sure would have loved knowing that within the next six months, there'd be a place for kids to go to—a safe place—no matter what was going on in their lives.

Liam and Jake had been stunned when Aidan told them what he planned to do. *Seriously? We thought we couldn't buy a place for at least another couple or three episodes. And even then, we were looking at something small.*

The house Aidan had bought wasn't small. It was an old five-bedroom place that had once been a shore house for fishermen, back at the turn of the last century. *It'll be big enough in case kids need to stay. We can hire a night manager. Get on the roster of approved emergency fosters.*

It would take another six months, at least. There were a million hoops to jump through, and the red tape piled up astronomically, but at some point, Ballard Youth would be a place for real, true hope. A home. Aidan was doing the work mostly by himself, an hour here and another hour there. Jake and Liam both helped when he needed extra hands, and some afternoons, he paid the fish boys to help with grunt work.

Tonight, he'd spent an hour ripping at lathe and plaster—he was widening a closet in a room that would eventually be a sixth bedroom. He'd only let himself work for an hour—Tuesday had made him promise to be home for a birthday dinner surprise.

Tuesday. Who needed a birthday surprise when he had her? Hopefully it would just be a plate of spaghetti and maybe a shot of good Scotch.

And her. Always her.

He pulled the truck to the curb and gazed up at the old Callahan house. His clothes hung in the master bedroom closet now, probably right where Mr. Brown's clothes had hung so many years before. Tuesday kept trying to put his name on the deed, but he wouldn't let her. *We've got two houses. Your name's on one, mine's on another. We'll live in this one for now.* It was good enough for him. The wedding band that he'd put on her hand last spring and its match that didn't leave his left hand—that was all he needed to be sure of her.

He glanced up at the top of the house as he walked to the door. The Missus Walk, as they called it, looked perfect. From it, Tuesday sometimes watched him fly.

But more often, she was with him, flying next to him. She had her own glider now and was intermediate rated.

And she had her own car, a small green hatchback.

She drove herself around town, white-knuckling it sometimes, but driving.

He opened the door. "I'm home!"

Nothing.

That was odd. Usually he was greeted by a happy laugh from the depths of the house. "Hello?"

Still nothing. The lights were out, and when he flipped the switch, nothing happened. Had the overhead light burned out again? He'd just replaced that bulb.

He made his way through the darkened living room and into the kitchen. "Tuesday?"

Aidan flipped on the light.

"*SURPRISE!*"

Everyone.

Absolutely everyone was there. His brothers, the network gang, everyone on his work crews. Tuesday's parents were there, to his surprise. The entire city council was there, as well as most of the police and fire department. Adele Darling was there with Nate—they must have closed the Golden Spike to get away. Norma, looking a bit odd so far from her perch at the saloon, hollered, "Happy birthday! I did a tarot reading for you and you would not *believe* what's in store for you!"

People roared with laughter, exulting in his look of honest surprise.

You didn't know?

Did you see your cake?

Marty parked right in front, and we knew you'd figure it out. You didn't figure it out?

Everyone was there but Tuesday. He accepted a glass of champagne and hugged his way through the packed kitchen. "Where's my wife?" God, he still liked saying that. "Anyone seen my wife?"

"Through here," Tuesday called. She was alone in the dining room, dimly lit by a single candle on the table top.

Wait. That wasn't their table. Their table was the big oval mahogany one that the network had bought. Neither of them liked it, but it was what they had, and it worked to hold up their dinner plates.

This one was bigger. Rectangular.

He flipped the light switch.

At first he could only see her. Red strappy dress, her hair curled and away from her face. Red lips. No makeup on her eyes, just that gorgeous brown gaze of hers, the one that reached his soul every time she laughed.

"Hi," he said.

"Hi, you." There was a file folder on the table in front of her. "I have two birthday gifts for you."

"I hope one of them is you."

"I have *three* birthday gifts for you." She pulled out the chair next to her. "The first is this table. Do you like it?"

Aidan grinned. "I really do. It's older than I thought we wanted, but it's good looking. It fits. It looks a lot like Mrs. Brown's old table, actually. How'd you manage that?"

Tuesday reached in front of him. She touched a scar in the wood.

It read *Caleb.*

"Holy..." It couldn't be. Aidan pushed his chair back with a clatter.

He dropped to the floor.

Above him, Tuesday laughed. "I knew you would do that next."

She knew, then, that he would already be sliding under the table. He had a small flashlight in his pocket, and he clicked the button to illuminate the underside of the table.

There, in faded yellow paint. *Aidan.*

He scooted back out. His nose stung, and his heart was so big he thought it might not fit in his chest anymore. "Where did you find this?"

"At the Episcopalian rummage sale."

"We went together."

"Remember I bought that vase? When I picked it up, I saw the name. I asked Henry to hold it for me. When I went back, I saw your name, and then I was sure."

Aiden took Tuesday's face in his hands. "You couldn't have given me a more precious gift." He kissed her. She tasted like mulled spice and happiness.

"I don't think that's true."

"No, really." He pulled back. "It's the best gift I've ever been given."

She touched the file folder on the table. "Open your other gift, then."

Aidan rubbed his chin, suddenly terrified he knew what was inside. "I can't."

"You can."

He searched her face, and found nothing but radiant joy. "Oh, my God."

She nodded, tears in her eyes.

The picture paper-clipped in the file was tiny, no more than two inches square. The baby had thin jet-black hair and dark eyes. She was lying on a tiny mattress, swaddled in a threadbare pink blanket.

He recognizer her, even though he'd never seen her before. *His daughter.* "The paperwork went through?"

Tuesday nodded. "I bought us the plane tickets to go pick her up. We leave at dawn. The orphanage will bring her to the legal consultant's office."

"Then she's ours?"

Tuesday nodded.

"Really, truly ours?"

Tuesday covered her mouth with a small sob. She nodded again.

Aidan pulled her to him then, and he didn't care that everyone else at the party had silently filed in to the dining room to watch. He kissed the top of Tuesday's robin-brown head. "What do you want to name her?"

Tuesday smiled up at him, tucking her hands into his front pockets. "Grace."

Of course. Tuesday's child was full of grace.

Their child.

He kissed her then, with no regard for the company watching. He'd have time to talk to them all later.

She kissed him back. And his heart flew.

ABOUT THE AUTHOR

Rachael Herron is the bestselling author of the novels *The Ones Who Matter Most, Splinters of Light,* and *Pack Up the Moon* (Penguin), the five-book Cypress Hollow series, and the memoir, *A Life in Stitches* (Chronicle). She received her MFA in writing from Mills College, Oakland. She teaches writing extension workshops at both UC Berkeley and Stanford and is a proud member of the NaNoWriMo Writer's Board. She's a New Zealand citizen as well as an American.

Rachael *loves* to hear from readers:
Website: rachaelherron.com
Facebook: Rachael.Herron.Author
Twitter: RachaelHerron
Email: Rachael@rachaelherron.com

Made in the USA
San Bernardino, CA
04 January 2018